WHERE
ARE MY GRAVES?

DEE DERRICK

HWD PUBLISHING

Published by:

HWD Publishing
Moretonhampstead, Devon, UK

Email: hwdpublishing@hotmail.com

First published in 2018

ISBN: 978-1-9996631-0-0

British Library Cataloguing-in-Publication Data
A catalogue record for this book is available from the British Library.

Typeset by Streamline Photography & Design, Uffculme, Devon.
Printed and bound by TJ International Ltd, Padstow, Cornwall

Front cover image: © Dee Derrick
Back cover image: © Dee Derrick

WHERE
ARE MY GRAVES?

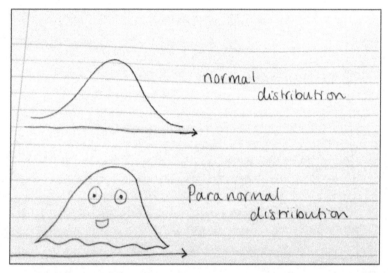

Thanks to friends who may recognise parts of themselves, the writer of the poetry, and for this endearing doodle found in a school folder

CONTENTS

PREFACE

The belief in reincarnation holds an interest for some, sits well with some, and not at all with others which is a perfect balance. No matter what you believe in you may recognise some aspects which apply to your own life. It may encourage you to wonder about things like "Why am I so afraid of closed doors?", "Why do I not like this particular house?" and, perhaps more likely, "Why do I not like that person over there who I have never met and probably never will?".

It will be hard, even for the most committed believer, to know that all the dreams in this story belong to one person and they are very real, as are the interpretations of them. This person did meet all the souls within them in their current lifetime and it took almost 40 years for it all to fall into place. The story which is wrapped around it incorporates fiction to make it more interesting but, rest assured, no-one was murdered during this latest incarnation.

A cautionary word...do not try to find your own past unless you are prepared to uncover things you might later wish had remained buried with your body. Results can be hard to handle.

CHAPTER ONE

Mayrie stood at the weir and tried to declutter her mind. She often visited here when things became a little difficult or crowded and it always amazed her how all that gushing water could bring such clarity. The weir was about a mile outside the village and this was one of her favourite walks although, when there was such beautiful scenery all around, how could any route be more preferred than another? There was the valley to the south, the weir to the east, the church and more of the older village houses to the north, whilst the west offered fields full of livestock.

Today though, something was different; the usual calming nature of the water rushing over the weir didn't work its magic. Mayrie felt tense, nervous – and looked around to see if she was alone. It felt very much as if there was someone else close by, watching, maybe lurking. Everything was still and the silence was unnerving. She stood without moving a muscle listening for any telltale sounds of twigs breaking, leaves rustling, footsteps – or breathing. Then she moved her eyes to look for movements, her head remaining perfectly still. Nothing.

She thought out loud, "Please protect me from all harm. If you are there, please grant me the armour of impenetrable protection; let it be above, below, front, back and to the sides of me with no cracks. In other words, please put me in a capsule of protection. Thank you."

Mayrie took a deep breath and blew out into the April air and a gust of wind swirled around her, gently blowing her long chestnut hair across her face. Within seconds she began to feel better and berated herself for being such a wuss and scared of thin air. There was no-one there. She stayed talking and listening to the water, mesmerised by its movement, speed and determination.

"All this water has to come from somewhere and go somewhere...I wonder who else it listens to on the way to the sea...who else it calms," she thought to herself.

Water, the keeper of life and the taker of life, the giver of fun and the maker of fear. The two sides of water. And that helped with her problem that day. Two sides...everything has two sides. Mayrie smiled, said thank you to the water and her place of sanctuary, turned and began to walk home the long way round, which meant following the river for a while.

"Ha! I shall see a short part of where the water comes from."

And then a question came to her.

"Why don't you do your family tree to see where you come from?"

"Good idea," she thought. "But I could do with some help now I've only really got gran left, and I'm not too sure how her memory is these days."

It was an hour later when Mayrie arrived home.

She began to speak out to the walls of her kitchen. "Right, house. How do I start doing my family tree? I'll tell you, shall I? Firstly, a cup of tea. Secondly, biscuits. Thirdly, I note down what I know. Fourthly, I'm going to ask gran one day soon."

The writing began and she wrote: Mayrie – parents Simon Nash and Millie Jones, brother Oliver, all deceased. Grandparents – Anna and Keiron Nash; Amber and Liam Jones.

Nash would be the easiest name to follow and Jones would be an absolute nightmare, so the visit to gran Jones was high on her to-do list. Tomorrow, Mayrie decided, she would visit gran and ask her about the Canadian side of the family.

Amber was sprightly for her 85 years and was not averse to expending energy. Today she'd decided to venture into the garage, home to many boxes of belongings which had not made it into the house when she moved there a couple of years ago. Her husband, Liam, had died five years ago – a heart attack brought on by the shock of losing their son-in-law, daughter and grandson in a freak accident when the lightning storms threw a fireball into their home, killing them instantly. No time to say goodbye; no time to say thank you; no time to say I love you. The pain and misery of it all was too much for Liam. Amber hung on to her mother's legacy of belief and tenacity and built her own strength from that so she could be there for her granddaughter who, apart from Amber, was now pretty much on her own. The family wasn't that small but it seemed to be because so many of them lived abroad. It was at times like these when feelings of sadness occurred because there weren't many around to reminisce with or to turn to when help was needed. Jack and Emily were in Canada, having moved there more than 60 years ago. Due to their ages it was certain they would not be back in this country again, although it seemed that there was every likelihood that her nieces and nephews would visit next year. She would probably never see her lovely brother and sister-in-law again and that made her very sad indeed. It was time to go hunting in the garage and reminisce with the boxes.

As she opened the door Mayrie called out, "Gran! Hello, gran...it's Mayrie...where are you?"

"In here, darling," came a voice from the garden room. "How have you been this week? Are you feeling a bit better now? Sore throats are so debilitating. Drink?"

Mayrie and her gran had always been close and it was an easy relationship that they shared. The wistful look in gran's eyes told Mayrie that she had been thinking about Jack and wishing she could see, touch and hug him. She'd been thinking about their mortality again which wasn't an outrageous thing given that Mayrie's parents and brother had been so abruptly taken from them not so many years ago, accentuating the fact that death was no respecter of age. Maybe talking about them would cheer her gran up and so the conversation started, Mayrie telling her about her plans to construct a family tree and asking for all the information possible.

It seemed no time at all before it was getting dark and cold and too late to start rooting around in the boxes for pictorial memories or any kind of documentation – if any existed – but then who needed actual documents. There were certainly documents from 60 years ago or so, but technology had improved vastly since those days and almost everything was on a database somewhere. It was so easy to speak a command and be provided with the information asked for, but right now it was time for Mayrie to go home. Gran was feeling so much happier for seeing her and together they had enjoyed a few happy hours reliving memories.

"Thanks for all your pointers gran. I'll go and record everything I can remember and make notes of what I want to find out next. The next two weeks are free for me now so, if you like, I could shift some of those boxes and maybe we can start turning them out. I'm a big strong girl now, you know," she said laughing.

"Thank you, darling, that would be really lovely. It will be nice to be able to get to them now, even if it does make me cry a little...but crying is good...it doesn't always mean sadness. Sometimes it can be an outpouring of love, just love."

Mayrie hugged gran tightly, kissed her cheek and made sure everything was all right with her before departing for her own home. She always felt sad when leaving but knew that gran valued her independence. The way she was going she probably would live to be over 100 and still be running around under her own steam and managing perfectly well.

On the way home, as Mayrie passed the weir, fingers of wind danced around her, swishing in her ears, and giving her a little shiver.

"Spring it may be," thought Mayrie. "But it feels like summer is still a fair way off."

The next morning Mayrie threw herself out of bed feeling energised and ready to take on the day. She felt almost excited as the anticipation of helping sort out gran's boxes flooded her mind. Dreams had pervaded her sleep and her whole being was buzzing with just about everything possible; it was odd that the dreams seemed so real and she remembered most of them with clarity. They made no sense at all, of course...names she didn't recognise from anywhere and faces, so many faces, a house and fashions that she knew were from decades ago. After breakfast she walked to the weir again out of desire to do so, not because she had a problem to muse over. The sun was shining and it was beautifully warm, leaves were showing new and green. She approached the weir and could hear the water tumbling well before she could see it. It sounded like music to her ears. It was beautiful, crystal clear music and for a moment she listened really hard. She had never noticed it sounding like that before, no doubt because she usually had problems to sort out when she went there and it gave no room for the lovely sound of the water to be truly heard. The sight was, as usual, calming and Mayrie stared at the designs the flowing water made. She blinked and looked around her, not quite sure what had happened but at the same time knowing that she had heard real music – a piece of music – a completely unknown piece of music. And she felt on the verge of tears.

"What on earth was that all about?" she threw out into the open.

The sounds of the water seemed to reply, "You'll see...you'll see...you'll see...you'll see."

A little puff of wind caressed her face and played with her ears, carefully disturbing her hair before going on its way. She checked the time to see how long she dared stay there before making her way to gran's house and couldn't believe that she had been there for 15 minutes already.

"Oh, I expect you had a little meditation, darling," gran said. "My mum and I used to do that quite a bit, especially when we needed to unwind. It was great – like in-depth daydreaming, in a way. I did it with your mum when she was growing up – did she do it with you?"

"No, gran, I don't remember her showing me how to meditate but she did tell me a little about it and told me about your spiritual beliefs but, if I think about it, she didn't seem to share them and I never asked you, did I?" questioned Mayrie.

"Well," answered gran. "I shall be happy to tell you anything you may want to know, if you are ever interested. It's not for everyone; each unto their own, as the saying goes."

Mayrie asked how to go into a meditation, what to expect and what would happen. Gran replied as simply as she could, but it wasn't a complicated thing anyway – really straightforward in fact.

"What you do," she began, "is get yourself calm enough to find that quiet place within...focus on something and try to block out all other thoughts – just like daydreaming when you can stare out of the window and your mind takes you to all kinds of places. By clearing any other thoughts it gives space for other stuff to come in. It could be profound words, faces, objects, colours, people, scenes. Let me give you an example of a simple one of mine. I was completely relaxed and these words came to me...the strength of a flower, the perseverance of a river and the endurance of a mountain...and I have remembered that for about 35 years."

"But what did it mean gran? I assume there was supposed to be a meaning?" queried Mayrie.

Amber folded her arms on the table and leaned forward slightly to answer. "Think how hard it must be for something as delicate as a flower to push its way through the ground, especially snowdrops in the frozen winter; that takes real strength. Then think about a river that keeps on and on, running to the ocean; that is perseverance. And now think of a mountain; flowers bloom and die, rivers change course and can dry up, but a mountain stays where it is through all weathers seemingly forever. That is endurance. If you think about our own lives and how often we may need to call on these qualities of strength, perseverance and endurance and then think about the flower, the river and the mountain you can see parallels. However frail we may seem, the strength is there somewhere to push through the problem – in the flower's case the frozen ground – however tired we may be we can go with the flow and even change the direction to get where we have to. And however tough the going seems to get we can just stand tall and still, like the mountain and withstand what we must."

Mayrie couldn't say anything for a moment and then very quietly, as she stared deep into Amber's eyes, "Teach me, gran, please teach me how to do it."

And so Amber sat with Mayrie, said a prayer of protection, and took her into a meditation. Once finished Amber asked her granddaughter if she had received anything. Tentatively Mayrie said she wasn't sure but there had been a piano, books, a man and a woman but she couldn't see their faces. Amber asked if it had felt like her mum and dad, or was it someone else she knew? Mayrie was disappointed to admit that she had no idea who they were.

When Mayrie asked gran to tell her what she had seen the answer was, "My mum came in to say hello, your grandad appeared and wanted me to tell you he is so proud of you. Then we had a bit of a conversation, and then I had...boxes! The boxes bit is because we are going to sort them out soon, unless it was telling me they are important. And I'm thinking that you probably picked up on my mum too because you saw a piano – she used to play the piano – did I ever tell you that?"

"I believe you did gran, a long time ago when I was little. Shall I make you a cup of tea and then, if you feel up to it, perhaps we could talk about Canada for a while?"

And that is precisely what they did. In fact, Mayrie gleaned a lot of information which fed her desire to construct a family tree enormously. That was it, she was well and truly hooked on the endeavour and she was going to enjoy the next two weeks.

CHAPTER TWO

They had turned out a 'Jack and Emily' box and really enjoyed talking about their younger days, including stories of when Amber had been little and how Jack had been a wonderful big brother to her. It was hard to believe that so many years had passed and they were now in the winter of their lives. Amber was 85 and Jack was 93 – or was he 95? Emily was two years younger than Jack. She had been a nurse, not for many a year now of course, and had seen many changes in medicine and healthcare. To go back in history and read about Florence Nightingale showed a frightening picture compared to today's medical advances. At that time the concern had primarily been for cleanliness and now it was more about what gran would call 'manufactured people.' In her youth there were various prosthetics and replacement joints such as knees and hips, but now that was viewed as old fashioned. The many wars that had blighted the world in the last 100 years had resulted in such dreadful injuries – some soldiers losing multiple limbs. This had been the catalyst for creating the reality of almost totally rebuilding a damaged body.

The meditation seemed to fire both Mayrie and Amber with enthusiasm for sorting the boxes. Amber felt warm and full of the love, which her mum and husband had brought through, and Mayrie was experiencing an excitement she didn't quite recognise. It was almost like the anticipation of at last opening a gift which had been teasing her for a week but somehow, quietly more intense. Whatever the feeling was it didn't quite make sense but she was going to enjoy it anyway.

"Use grandad's sack trucks darling," said gran. "And bring the next one into the living room. It will be more comfy to turn it out here."

Five minutes later gran heard, "Here we are gran, another 'Jack and Emily' box. What treasures have you got in here?"

They set about turning it all out so that Amber could tell Mayrie as many tales of great uncle Jack and great aunt Emily as they both could stand which, in the event, turned out to be a lot. There were old photographs in albums and memory sticks for plugging into a computer, as gran put it. It was brimful of pictures of everything that made up their life in Canada; their home, their children, and some pictures of them with gran when she had been out to see them, and more of when they had been over to see gran. Mayrie had met Jack and Emily every time they had been over to England, the last time being ten years ago. It was a shame that they hadn't been able to be here for the funerals of her parents, brother and grandad; she would love to see them again but she didn't want to talk about that as it might make gran sad because they all knew it was most unlikely that they would be coming to England again. Poor gran. She and Jack had always been very close even with the miles between them. He had filled the role of their dad who had left them when they were quite young and Jack had looked after his much younger sister with great affection and love. All these old memory sticks...how sad that they weren't compatible with today's technology. Mayrie's thoughts started to churn and possibilities were forming; she would speak to Anni – her brother, Roshan, was a technical whizz and he might have some ideas.

"Gran? Did you like Canada? You've been several times so I guess it must have been OK," asked Mayrie.

"It's a lovely place darling, but we could never quite make that decision to leave England after mum died," replied gran, diverting her gaze to the window. She sighed, straightened her back, pursed her lips as if steeling herself to continue. "Mum was only in her 50s when she died. It made us realise how short and cruel life can be so, although we had been in Canada for a year and intended to make a life there, we decided to return to England to spend time with grandad's parents. Then your mum and uncle Dylan came along, and everything just snowballed when they made their own friends and started school. Then, of course, grandad's parents were getting older, and then grandad found out his heart was not in the best shape so the time never seemed right to up sticks and make such a major move."

"Do you ever wish that you had moved to Canada gran?"

"Sometimes, yes," she said with a faraway look in her sparkly eyes. "But grandad and I never regretted for one moment staying here. Had we emigrated we would probably have been wracked with guilt at taking the children away from their friends and grandparents, and leaving the grandparents with a gaping hole in their lives. As you know, grandad didn't have any brothers or sisters so his mum and dad would have had a very lonely time. Even so, and this seems a strange thing to say, yes, I do wish we had gone to Canada to live. An odd situation to be in, isn't it? Wishing we had emigrated, yet not regretting staying here. Never mind, too late now. Jack and I have good contact."

Mayrie thought she saw a tear slip down Amber's cheek but said nothing when her gran made for the kitchen calling, "Tea, darling?"

As she went, her hand dipped into her pocket to take out a tissue.

That evening Mayrie's thoughts were still fighting for first place in the line-up of importance. She chose the simplest one first and contacted Anni to ask if she thought Roshan would mind her picking his technical brain. Anni was interested to hear why and gave her a contact point for her brother in London without hesitation. "Strike whilst the iron is hot" she could imagine her gran saying as she said, "Andante, please deliver the following message to Roshan Bhakta at 95AZ7342NW10:

"Hello Roshan, my name is Mayrie Nash. I work with your sister, Anni, and she said you wouldn't mind if I contacted you with some technical questions, so I hope you don't. Long story, very boring, but I am turning out old boxes of my gran's possessions and I have found some old memory sticks, containing loads of photographic memories of her brother. What I would like to know is, is there a way of getting to see the pictures stored on these sticks? What is the possibility of old computer stuff having any compatibility with today's systems? Sorry to bother you. Any help you could give is very much appreciated. Thank you."

The voice came back, "Message delivered. May I help further?"

To which Mayrie replied, "No, that's all for the moment, Andante, thank you."

The magenta light shone from a thin, flat piece of metal no bigger than the palm of a woman's hand, dimming to a gentle glow.

Then she set about the next thought vying for attention. It took a little while to sort it out but she was very happy when a possible solution was found. The other little matter would necessitate contacting her employers tomorrow and that could be done first thing in the morning before the real work of the day began. There was always that 30-minute grace period when everyone got themselves sorted out, caught up with any leftover messages from the day before, or had that almost compulsory coffee which seemed to be a tradition that had lasted forever. Mayrie was ready for bed when she heard a ding and saw the increasing magenta light in the corner of the room denoting an incoming message so, bed put to one side for the moment, she spoke into the room.

"I see you have a message for me, Andante – please tell me."

The magenta voice answered, "Yes, from Roshan Bhakta. The message is: Hello, Mayrie, this is Roshan. No, I don't mind at all – my sister has spoken of her colleagues so I vaguely know who you are – always pleased to help any friend of Anni's but I would need to see the stuff you have before I can say what may or may not be done. Have you got anything else? The old systems are fascinating so, actually, I'd love to help you out. I heard yesterday that I am being sent down your way next week and will be staying with Anni for a couple of weeks – suppose I should let her know – so, if it would be all right with you, perhaps you could show me the things then?"

As always, Andante asked, "May I send a reply for you?"

Excitedly, Mayrie said, "Yes please Andante. Please convey that this would be wonderful, Roshan, thank you. Haven't found anything else yet but we are only on the second box. It is very interesting turning out gran's stuff...some of it goes back...well, possibly 100 years! She has things which belonged to her mother, and she would be 117 years old now. Wow! I'm getting even more excited now I am saying it. I'll wait to hear from you when you arrive at Anni's. Big thanks. Thank you Andante."

Within seconds there was another ding and Andante reported, "No problem Mayrie. If you find anything else interesting let me know. This is intriguing."

When Mayrie was excited about something, sleep did not arrive very quickly. She tossed this way and that, got up again and paced around her home, ate a piece of cake and then tried again. Better, but not good enough. That is when the thinking began and her mind was filled with Jack, Emily and their family, and Winnipeg. A winning combination, it sent Mayrie to sleep and the dreams were filled with all the things she had learned that day, giving her a magical night's sleep. As usual, when she was excited Mayrie flung herself out of bed very early in the morning, feeling ready to take on the world. She had to wait to speak to her employers but she was pleased with the result and, as soon as that was over, she started the journey to her gran's home and decided to stop at the weir to breathe in the beauty of it and to feel its excitement, which seemed equal to her own. Strange how it could be both exciting and calming at the same time. A lock of hair blew across her face and tickled her chin, then a twiggy branch of a tree played with the back of her neck.

"See you tomorrow weir," she called out, feeling slightly foolish for having done so, but at the same time feeling as if she was talking to an old friend.

Amber and Mayrie turned out several boxes over the next few days. There were more memory sticks, some photographs and DVDs; it would be great when Roshan came down to stay with Anni. Turning out the box entitled 'Our Wedding' brought back so many wonderful memories for Amber, not to mention new knowledge for Mayrie to include in her family tree. Some of the photographs were clear but again a lot of the stuff was on memory sticks, discs and even a digital camera in the box, which would have held a memory card. Unfortunately, it no longer worked. The batteries would be long dead gran had said. Never mind, Roshan was coming. There was one photo of a group of people which Mayrie had seen before; it was always in the drawer at gran and grandad's house and she would ask to look at it sometimes because it was interesting to see all the old fashions and hairstyles.

"Gran – Can you remember who all these people are in this photo?" she asked Amber.

"I'm not sure darling, but I hope so. Let me have a look. Well, that is me and grandad, of course, and that is grandad's mum and dad – lovely people, they were," she answered, gently touching the images of their faces. "And there is your great grandma, my mum, standing with Jack and Emily; they stayed here for two months then. These were neighbours and I'm sad to say I cannot remember their names...this lady was called Frances, this was Alison I believe, and this is George. I first knew George when we were three...and this is James and Megan, also my friends," she concluded.

"I love all the different styles of clothes gran...there are long dresses, short dresses, trousers, high heels, flat shoes, long hair, short hair, hats, no hats," commented Mayrie, marvelling at all the different colours and styles. "Tomorrow, can we look at your mum's boxes, gran?" And that is what they did. There were four boxes in all and Mayrie felt as if she would burst if she had to wait any longer to get to the really old stuff.

As usual Mayrie had tea with her gran before going home. Every evening was offering a little more light, especially when it had been a sunny day like today, so to stop at her sanctuary was a definite yes. Mayrie stood in her usual place and gazed all around, taking in all the beauty which she never grew tired of. Then, the strangest of things, she thought someone had walked close to her but, turning to see who it was, saw no-one. Many times before she had imagined she'd heard a car drive past behind her but there was never anything there; it was just one of those places where noises happened. Noises happened at work sometimes and no-one took any notice of them, although she had to admit that whenever she had mentioned it most people looked at her blankly, silently expressing that they thought she was from another planet.

"Hey weir, guess what gran and I are doing tomorrow? We are going to go into the oldest boxes. I can't wait to see what we find in there," she said out loud and, as she turned to leave, shadows were beginning to appear as the light changed. Actually, that did give her a small jolt because, for a moment, it could have been mistaken for a person standing beside the tree. Mayrie laughed at herself and, saying goodbye to the weir, headed for home.

On arrival she was pleasantly surprised to see the increasing glow of magenta heralding a message arriving and was even more delighted to hear Andante report: "Hello,

Mayrie...it's Roshan. How are you getting on with the boxes? I will be down with Anni on Friday night, so maybe we can meet up over the weekend. Have you found anything else yet?"

Her reply was immediate: "Oh good! We are tackling the oldest boxes tomorrow so goodness knows what is in them. So far we have more memory sticks, some DVDs and a digital camera with a dead battery, so we don't know what secrets the card may hold. It sounds silly but I am becoming very excited about these boxes. Oh my! It is Wednesday today...we had better get a move on. Looking forward to meeting you, Roshan, and thank you very much indeed for saying you will take a look at these things."

Ding. "Not a problem. I'm actually looking forward to it myself. Speak to you soon."

Thursday arrived in the dark for Mayrie who, by her own admission, like a small child waiting for Father Christmas to arrive, was up at 4am. It really made no difference at all because she took delight in watching the dawn break and the sun start to rise. Of sunrise and sunset, sunrise had always been Mayrie's favourite to watch, even before losing her family in the freak accident. Sunset made her feel as though she was losing them all over again but sunrise was the promise of a brand new day, bringing a wealth of new things.

If she started the day feeling like that, it made her feel not quite invincible but very strong and in control of her life. She gave her home a 'lick and a promise' as her gran would say, with a quick tidy and clean up and more or less putting everything back where it should be. Hair washed, smelling nice and donning old clothes in anticipation of grappling with the four old boxes at the back of the garage, Mayrie set off to see her gran. She was really enjoying this time off work and so was gran – that was obvious. To spend all this time together was wonderful and to share gran's life more fully was a gift. It had always seemed a little one-sided with gran knowing everything about Mayrie...watching her grow as a pregnancy, her birth, first steps, first words, school, absolutely everything; yet Mayrie didn't really know much about gran's life. Gran had not been one to go on about herself but she was otherwise an outgoing person. She would talk about Jack, grandad and mum a lot but never much about just her; it was always about someone else and her but rarely just about her, just gran's way. That is probably what set her apart from most people...nothing was ever only about her...always about others.

The first thing to do at gran's needed no thought – have a cup of tea and a second breakfast – then clear some serious space for the first box.

"We couldn't keep everything," said gran. "But I kept things that were of sentimental value. Her jewellery, her books and probably some stuff that could have been thrown away."

As Amber opened the first box a smile spread across her face and then she chuckled. Then she laughed uncontrollably until tears rolled down her soft face. Mayrie was left to do no other than to watch and eventually fall victim to the infectious laughter of her gran and she, too, fell apart at the seams. It was a while before they settled down and Amber unwrapped the flat object roughly the size of a dinner plate.

"Oh, gran! Why are you laughing about a clock?" giggled Mayrie.

"Look at it, darling. Oh, this clock caused so much hilarity. This was my mum's – your great grandma's – humour. And I know what else is in this box too," puffed gran as she tried so hard to calm down, although she didn't really want to. This was fun.

"What about it?" asked Mayrie, and then she realised and screeched with amusement. "The numbers run backwards."

"Yes, and the hands went backwards too, so it always told the time correctly, it just meant that whoever was looking at it had to be able to mirror read. We all got so used to it that it became difficult to read a right-way-round clock in the end," explained gran. "Mum showed me how to mirror write as well. In fact, one day when she took me to school the teacher wasn't in the room and we were all being loud and not really behaving, so she picked up the pen and wrote on the board 'please sit quietly until Mrs. Evans comes back.' But she wrote it in mirror writing and, believe it or not, we all stopped dead in our tracks and watched her do it. Possibly the most interesting thing was that we all seemed to be able to read it quite easily. The class loved mum and no-one ever turned down an invitation to our house for a birthday party. Ha! The games she got us to play! The jelly game...she would make a jelly so that it was very wobbly...two children sat opposite each other, cross-legged on the floor, blindfolded, and were given a bowl of jelly and a spoon each. They had to feed each other. My word! The mess we used to make...and she never minded. As long as we were having fun she was happy. I remember one time Frankie, that was mum's friend, came to a party. Of course, I realised when I was older that the birthday parties were dual purpose; the children had theirs and mum had one for the parents going on at the same time. Anyway, Frankie came and Jack was there too, and Frankie picked up a Tunnocks Tea Cake, a really squidgy marshmallow encased in chocolate on a biscuit base. I shall always remember this – Frankie put it on the palm of her hand and looked at it, then she looked at Jack, looked back at the Tunnocks and, as quick as a flash, splatted it on his forehead. It went everywhere and everyone was rendered incapable with laughter, especially Jack."

Mayrie, by this time, was rocking with mirth and begging Amber for more such tales, which tumbled out throughout the morning. The next thing they unwrapped was a garden ornament, a gnome.

"So, what's the story behind this one gran?" asked Mayrie.

"Well, mum was always one for the unusual. If most people hated it, she loved it, and garden gnomes fell into that category. She didn't have many come the end, but this was the best one so I kept him. Oh, look what is with him, I'd quite forgotten about this. When your mum was small she found this stone and carried it around everywhere with her. She used to call it her pet rock...so it was kept. This is yours now darling, here you are."

Amber lovingly handed over the pet rock to Mayrie. When Mayrie fell silent and looked as though she might cry, Amber thought it was not a bad idea to lift the mood.

"She also used to run around with earthworms in her pockets or in her fists. We had a devil of a job to make her let them go," Amber said with such a straight face that Mayrie had no option but to laugh out loud.

"Drink, darling?" asked gran, who was already on the way to the kitchen and wiping away an errant tear as she went. "Plenty of biscuits I think too," she added quietly.

The tea break was welcome and they spent their time chatting about a certain small girl with blonde curly hair tied up in bunches, a small girl who wore denim dungarees, hoodies and wellies. A small girl who had a brother who loved to stamp in cowpats and say, "Smells good mum." That same brother who would take his sister by the hand and play dirt-tracks with her. These two small children who would smile at their mum at the end of the day, happy to be dirty from head to toe whenever possible. These two children, Millie and Dylan, who happened to become Mayrie's mother and uncle. Amber had often thought she might just as well have had two boys but decided that having a girl who acted as though she was a boy was probably more fun.

The second box came in and what a treasure chest it turned out to be, full of the technology of the day. Amber knew what all the things were called. There was a laptop, an MP3, an iPad, another digital camera, something that Amber said was a digital picture frame, CDs, a mobile phone and a hand-held Dictaphone. This, intriguingly, contained a cassette and some other loose cassettes as well. Roshan was going to have a field day. It was unlikely any of it worked because things were probably so different now. If that wasn't exciting enough, the third and fourth boxes contained books. Some were journals, some were music books, and some were reading books all by the same author, Margot Mogford.

"Close your mouth, darling," laughed Amber. "You'll catch flies like that."

"But, gran, you've just told me that great grandma was 'Margot Mogford'. I didn't know she had been a writer, and a fairly successful one by the look of it," gasped Mayrie.

"I don't think she wrote any more after I went to University, don't really know why, except that she had an accident during my studying years. As soon as I graduated grandad and I married and went over to Canada with the intention of spending a few years with Jack and Emily and then, when we came back to England, we stayed here."

"Look at this, gran...two pieces of poetry...they are lovely...listen...this first one is called Reflections."

REFLECTIONS

So sad, little boy. Feeling unloved and unwanted?

In the way, a nuisance? Wished elsewhere every day?

Don't you belong there, little boy?

With your sibling, your mum and your dad?

Feel you don't make the grade expected

To make you one of them?

But you do, lad, you do!

If only you knew. If only you could see

What you have, what you bring...

Who you will grow to be.

Working hard, young man?

Struggling to fit in with them all,

To show them you have earned

And deserve approval at least.

You made the grade, young man,

And excelled in your chosen career,

But still you feel a longing

For what you hold most precious, most dear.

You have worked hard, young man,

And have much loved babes of your own.

Yet still you are looking for that

Which you thought never became yours.

Stop hurting, lovely man.

Don't you know where it is? Can't you see?

They couldn't give you what you already were.

It was there all the time. Face the mirror and say

I see kindness. I see love. I see me.

"And then there is this one...it's called In the Face of Death."

IN THE FACE OF DEATH

The gentle touch of his hand, the soft light in his eyes,

The whispered words...they all spoke of love.

He said, "I want to sleep now – my heart is full – I am not afraid."

Then his soul knocked on the door of relief and the voice of his Lord said,

Come, Andrew...time to come home.

Relinquish your life's armoury...come home.

The battle of life isn't easy, nor was it ever meant to be.

At times you will have found it unjust or cruel unnecessarily.

You have carried courage, strength and fortitude,

And shouldered well adversity, fear and dread.

And whether asleep or awake you have received and given,

Gifts of love, loyalty, respect, and that of a friend.

This war you have fought wasn't to harm or destroy;

It was for loving and living, acceptance, taking and giving.

You have done well, Andrew, your achievements great.

Your time is here, Andrew; put down your life's weapons.

Heaven's arms await you...

Come home.

He smiled as he shook hands with eternity, free from
pain upon pain,
And closed his eyes to this life for the very last time.
So find a smile for yourself, and be happy for him...
That he is at peace...at home...where he needed to be.

"Gran, these are lovely. I wonder who wrote them? Do you...
gran? Are you all right? Gran?"

Mayrie was upset to see her gran was silently crying and
trying very hard to disguise that fact. "What is it, gran?"

Amber wiped away the tears, cleared her throat and with
a voice choked with emotion said, "Mum wrote that and read
it at Andrew's funeral."

Mayrie didn't want to ask who Andrew was because
tears were still copiously falling from Amber's eyes. Whoever
he was, he must have been someone important to her,
someone she had cared very much about. The tears were,
indeed, tears of deep sorrow – sorrow that Amber hadn't
understood properly all those years ago and wished with all
her being that her ego hadn't blinkered her view of the reality
of others' happiness back then. Why couldn't she have just
accepted the situation...had the courage of blind faith? It had
been explained to her but she didn't want to see it then – her
bias had been too strong. All Amber could do now was to hold
on to the knowledge that she did eventually understand

everything her mother had told her and they had made their peace. However, she would never lose the underlying knowledge that, thanks to her and Jack, her mum probably didn't have the complete joy she should have had. Amber excused herself from the room and returned fifteen minutes later ready to continue.

The last box offered up a huge surprise. As Mayrie turned it all out to have a jolly good look she found what looked like a manuscript, which she began to read. Then she read the beginnings of the books penned by 'Margot Mogford' and found that none of them began that way.

"Gran, I think we may have the manuscript of a book she started to write but never had published...look!" said Mayrie with both excitement and apprehension in her voice.

She dug a little deeper and found another much shorter manuscript and began to read that one too. Her interest straining at the leash, Mayrie put them both to one side with the intention of reading them as soon as possible, for instance tonight, if gran would let her take them home...which she did. The journals could wait for a moment.

The evening started with an excited message to Roshan.

"Roshan...it's Mayrie. You'll never believe what we have found. We have a laptop, an MP3 player, mobile phone, dictaphone plus tapes, CDs, digital cameras and a digital photo frame, more memory sticks and an iPad. I feel guilty putting all this on you and I don't want you to feel you have to look at all of it but if you would like to choose one or two things that would be lovely."

It wasn't many minutes before Andante related Roshan's reply: "How wonderful – this is absolutely amazing. I would very much like to look at all of it, if I may. This stuff interests me a lot...can't wait to see it all. Maybe Anni could bring me to see you on Saturday, if you will be around, then we can go through it all and I can make a start."

And so it was arranged that Anni and Roshan would go to see Mayrie on Saturday.

Gran was happy for Mayrie to take all the things for Roshan to look at and even confessed to feeling excited at the thought of what would be seen, what old memories would be reawakened and what may be discovered. So on Friday things were packed up again ready to be taken to Mayrie's home.

"Gran, would you like to come and stay the weekend with me?" asked Mayrie. "And then you can meet the guy who is going to help with this...and I would love to have you."

Amber thought about it and accepted. A change of scenery would be lovely. On the way home gran asked if they could stop at the weir because she hadn't been there for a very long time.

"I grew up near here, you know," said gran. "We stayed here for a while before grandad and I settled in Gloucester. It's only since grandad died that I have been back to this area. Isn't it beautiful?"

As they stood watching the water crashing over the rocks they both suddenly turned their heads together to look at the same spot.

Amber smiled and quietly said, "Hello mum."

"Can you feel her, gran?" asked Mayrie and was rather shocked by her answer.

"I can see her, darling...can't you?"

"I can see shadows by the trees, gran, but that's all."

"Look harder, Mayrie. Can't you see legs, arms and a head at least? Just empty your mind, look at the shadow and ask to be shown."

After a couple of minutes Mayrie took a sharp breath in, put her hand to her mouth, looked at her gran and whispered, "Yes...I see...someone...someone who is not old but not young like me...can't see it clearly enough to see a detailed face but I'm sure it is a woman. Oh, gran, this is intriguing."

They talked for a long time that night about what they had seen, about spiritualism, about all the old technical wizardry of the time that had been found in the boxes. Then Mayrie began to read the largest manuscript entitled 'Consider This' to her gran so that they could both experience it at the same time.

CHAPTER THREE

CONSIDER THIS

Consider this. The question I have asked myself for years is 'what is the spark of life – where does it come from?' Thinking about conception, you have ovum and sperm; each has life, they meet, they fuse, there is still life but what actually makes it grow into a viable child? Even when they fuse sometimes they die and an early miscarriage occurs – the life created by the two halves does not come to fruition. The moment of fusion is the vortex for the soul to enter. If the soul doesn't come through then life does not progress. I have concluded that the soul is the spark of life and without it there is no life.

That life, that soul, brings with it memories – like a form of blueprint, or a computer hard drive that is not full. There is much capacity for new information, new happenings, but still there is the old memory which will be the foundation for the life now beginning to grow. It is a new life with old beginnings; beginnings that won't be remembered unless the human form is either lucky, or unlucky, enough to remember. It is not always good to know what has gone before. If you want to find out be prepared to accept whatever you discover. If you are not prepared, and you find out, you face a difficult time reconciling yourself with it.

We all know everything has two sides. There's a back, a front, an inside, an outside; heads and tails of a coin; light and dark; fat and thin; you name it and there will be an opposite, and so it is with life. With life there comes death, with death there comes life – can you hear your mother or grandmother saying, 'One in the family dies and another comes in.' So there it goes, round and round and round. Things have a habit of coming back into our lives; we meet new people with new situations; we don't even know who they are but there are signs. I'm telling you, there are signs and when you have to know something those signs will whack you, sometimes almost literally, until you sit up and take notice.

We have all met someone and thought, 'Wow! I like this person – I'm really going to get on with them.' And yet on meeting another, maybe just walking down the street with not a clue who they are, you've never seen them before and not likely to again, yet from the first glance you think, 'I do NOT like that person one bit.' How can we make decisions like that from a glance? Well, something is coming round and telling you, whacking you. If there is unfinished business it will follow you and there will be no getting away from it. Whether it is good or bad, if it's unfinished business it will find you. If you run from it and miss the chance it offers, your soul will have to come back and try again. It will be relentless. That's life – up, down, sometimes sideways but always backwards and forwards. It is sad and happy, dull and exciting; life is the whole package. Death is the only certainty. Then again, what is death? I think death is the time when the computer hard drive is full and it's time to go away and declutter – take away all the unnecessary trappings of daily life, all those shopping trips to Morrisons and so on; the important things stay – the love, hate, fun, dismay, despair – all the emotional stuff stays. Just imagine, after a number of lifetimes we would all be gibbering wrecks unless we sort it out, whatever 'it' is, during ensuing lifetimes. What happens if we have nothing left to sort out and there is nothing else to do? I don't know for sure but I think we go somewhere else and start helping from another side – we get to look over others, guide and protect them if we can. It's just another whole new level when we've finished on earth. I have no idea what to expect when I've finished...it is daunting but I have the very real feeling that this is my last earthly incarnation. Too much is happening, I'm meeting too many people, too many things are being put in front of me to resolve. Maybe I'd cause too much trouble if I had another lifetime here. Ha! Who knows? Well, someone will if I don't get everything done in this one. Best get a move on.

She read her words back to herself. Having believed in reincarnation since she was able to think, this explained a lot. She had always felt others could not understand what she was thinking or feeling and certainly never why. Well, now – after all this time – she finally understood. All the times she was hurt by such comments as 'you're not normal, you,' now meant nothing and the hurt truly replaced by a smile. Ha! Normal? Who was normal? What was normal? Was normal the state of living in ignorance of all that had gone before, or was normal living in the state of knowing exactly what had gone before?

If only she had been able to tell her father before he died that she knew who he was, who he had been, understood his soul's pain – and her own at last. If only she could have told him how she had tried to come back to him, to find the father she had been denied. She held his hand as he passed from this world into the next at 35 minutes into the day of Sunday 31 March 2013. At that moment something in her died too, a phrase so often used and one which she disliked intensely, but what had died was the driving need to fit that last piece of a jigsaw. That part of her present and very distant past had been sorted out. That part of her purpose in this life had also been sorted.

Buzz buzz. The sound of Beth's mobile made her jump a little and she thought that perhaps to turn the volume down would be a good idea. That done, she read the short message;

"Hi B. Going to Church tomorrow? It will be nice to chat again. J."

She smiled to herself.

"Hi J. Yes, will be there barring accident, illness or death. Got more to say since Thursday? B."

Buzz buzz. "I enjoyed our group's coffee morning on Thursday. It is a welcome social event for me. Looking forward to seeing you tomorrow. J."

"I thoroughly enjoy them too...don't go very far with mother being as she is...a welcome distraction. I have a friend who pops in most Saturdays for a chat and catch up, so I don't do too badly. Will be glad when Charlotte gets back. B."

Buzz buzz. "I expect you worry a lot more than you let on; it is difficult to have that most precious thing, a child, out of your care – even if she is almost 18. Have a good time with your friend when she – she? he? – arrives. See you tomorrow. J."

"Yes, she. No doubt we will talk for England! B."

Buzz buzz. "No doubt. J."

Beth's social calendar wasn't overflowing with events; she usually met her friends from the meditation group for coffee once a week. Most Sundays she went to church – that's where she and James crossed paths – and, of course, there were the meditation evenings, a wonderful exercise in relaxation. On a few occasions during this she had found herself looking down from a mountain over the top of thick forestation, the treetops looking suspiciously like an enormous piece of broccoli. Further in the distance was a mountain on both the left and right with what looked like ocean between them confirmed, she thought with her own brand of dry humour, by a ship sailing on it. She often wondered if such a place existed. James hadn't joined the meditation group; perhaps it wasn't his thing. Beth could ask.

She thought about James. He was such a nice man, so kind. So easy to talk to and such pleasant company. There was something about him that reminded her of Mark. It wasn't a physical likeness; whereas Mark was about 5' 9" tall, had shortish blond hair and an athletic build with strong arms and large hands, James was taller at probably 6'. He had sandy hair fashioned in such a way that it made Beth think of a high-flying businessman, a physique which was gently rounded all over and hands that were definitely not those of a man employed in outdoor work. Ah, Mark, she thought, as she let out a sigh. Now, there was a blast from the past; she hadn't really thought hard about him for a long while now. The hurt and turmoil had settled for her at least. She'd heard that he and Sarah had moved in together and all seemed to be well, so that made her happy. It dawned on her that, actually, her father had been the second piece of jigsaw of life to fall into place – Mark had been the very first, and what a story that has turned out to be. The dream was not the full story, only a small part of it. In the dream Mark had been a soldier, and she a well-dressed lady at a ball. It was knowledge that, as always coming from nowhere, he was going off to battle within a day or two. And a lady watching him from the top of the short stairway leading into the room was Beth's soul in another lifetime. Her beautiful peacock blue gown shone like satin and there was unfinished business between them so obviously symbolised by the tacking stitches around the hem of the gown. The knowledge told her that the soldier didn't return from battle, leading to great heartache for the young woman.

Beth's mind took her back to when she took a part-time evening clerical job. She was not allowed to talk about it and necessitated swearing the Official Secrets Act, making it all sound so terribly important, but it entailed only filing documents for a Government department. It was a job which somehow just fell into her lap, with every circumstance being perfect when, on paper, it really shouldn't have worked at all. Michael had long gone and Daniel was 16 and happy to look after Charlotte for the 12 hours a week that Beth worked. How blessed she was to have two children who adored each other and got along so well. Actually, Daniel was so pleased to have a sister because Beth and Michael had elected for a termination when Daniel was only three. They had explained to him that the baby in her tummy was very poorly and the doctors wouldn't be able to make it better and so, although it made them really very sad, the baby wouldn't be born after all and he wouldn't have his brother or sister at the promised time. He had put his little hand on Beth's arm, looked into her eyes and said, "Don't worry, mum; I'm going to tell the doctor that we are going to try again."

How she didn't cry she didn't know, and where had he got that? Because they had not even considered trying again, let alone talked about it. What an amazing child and now, here he was, an amazing adult. The decision they'd made was based on a complete overview of their situation; it was all very well for the pro-lifers and the pro-abortionists with their very clear-cut ideas, but what about when there are things in the way that make up what was fashionably called 'the grey area'? The grey area was huge but even if you yourself were a pro-lifer, what if to bring one life in to a family threatened that of another? Daniel's asthma was triggered by stress amongst other things so whichever way it was looked at he would either suffer stress because of a very poorly baby that could easily die within the first 12 months of life, or the stress of seeing his baby brother or sister being given up for adoption. He had already been taken to hospital four times that year with severe asthma attacks. The darkness of that situation followed Beth until only recently when the story of one of her dreams had been revealed to her. Now she could, perhaps, live a little happier with it. That had been the third piece of the jigsaw. Her dad had been the second, but what of the first – Mark? She wondered where he was and what he was doing now. They had been so very close at one stage and she went back to the first night he came to work at the document archives. It was a fairly boring sounding job but it was actually quite fun. The whole operation covered the entire South West and occupied several buildings. That was a lot of documents. The three new recruits were introduced and Beth was asked to train Mark. The second she saw him her brain said, "What a strange place for you to be." This didn't seem to be an odd thought at all until a little later she realised that she'd never seen him before in her life. That was a bizarre beginning to an even more bizarre friendship. Or was it a relationship? Close call...which? From the very moment of meeting it really was as though they had known each other forever. They finished off each other's sentences; spoke the same words at the same time, always ended up working as a pair no matter how they resolved to work with different partners. Something would then happen that meant they ended up in a pair again. Even when it came to checking files against their computer printouts one of them would have 'Hand' and the other would have 'Foot' or some such equivalent. Everything about them was identical or linked. They shared a strong fascination for Egypt, opinions, likes and dislikes. There was, indeed, an enormous bond between the two of them – this young man 17 years her junior and her, a mother of two. It turned out that Mark was a farmer so, yes; it was a strange place for him to be.

They seemed to be in some kind of private life that no-one else could share, not because they didn't want them to, but because they just couldn't get into it. After only three days they were asked how long they had known each other to which Beth automatically replied, "Hundreds of years." And, not a nanosecond later, Mark had replied, "Something like that." As he said those three simple words the wide smiles left their faces for a brief moment and their eyes met, conveying the message 'I see you' and, for some strange reason, a dream of long ago which she'd not been able to dispel flashed through her mind. It had been of a harbour scene with black, choppy seas around and all that could be seen was a character very similar in appearance to Darth Vader of Star Wars fame facing two others. One was a girl and the other a human aside from his head – definitely a male the unspoken knowledge said – and his head was that of a crocodile. It made no sense at all, so why did she remember it?

Soon after that Beth knew that she and Mark had been brought together for some special reason, but all she could work out was that she had a job to do for him; she had to lead him somewhere and leave him there, stand back and let him go. Oooo, that was going to be difficult because with every passing day they seemed to be getting more and more exclusive to one another and yet...and yet...there was no socialising outside of work, no physical contact, not even a playful tap on the shoulder or brushing of hands as they grappled with the paperwork and so on. What were the chances of not touching at all when they worked so closely? Everyone else touched in some small way Beth noticed, but the pair of them never, ever, actually touched. She imagined putting her palm to his and what followed frightened her as she knew, as always from nowhere, that if they ever touched the pain would be like a physical kick to the heart and the emotional pain would be nothing short of torture.

After four months Mark decided to become a permanent member of staff – his dad had decided to retire from farming and the economic climate was not favourable to farmers, so when Mark saw his chance he took it. There were good prospects as a civil servant and he was young enough to get promotions and make something of himself in that job. As a permanent staff member Mark had to work days. Beth would miss him terribly but by now they were texting or speaking on the phone on the days they didn't work together, and even some of the days they did. It was all about nothing in particular – his parents, the farm, Daniel, Charlotte, the car going in for its MOT, lots of laughter – but nothing in particular. Certainly no covert lovey-dovey stuff. They didn't have that, even though they thought the world of each other and they just chatted and chatted as though making up for lost time. To people looking in at them it certainly seemed as though they were in a deep relationship, but that all the kissing and cuddling was kept for behind closed doors. At the end of his last night shift everyone said their goodbyes to this very popular co-worker and without a second thought he and Beth shared a huge hug, which had a devastating effect but, in the event, didn't actually surprise Beth at all. The moment her ear touched Mark's face she experienced what could only be described as a bomb exploding in her head, but only that side of her head. There was a very clear defining line running from the forehead to the nape of her neck and the pain did not cross that line. That pain lasted for several days and her GP could offer no explanation, his only possible immediate course of action was to then prescribe strong painkillers. He suggested a diagnosis of acute sinusitis but even he didn't believe it to be right. Beth knew. It was because she and Mark had touched. It hadn't affected him, so what was it all about?

As time passed she was slowly, but increasingly, feeling unwell. Nothing specific aside from tiredness, more pains from the dreadful adhesions in her abdomen, lack of concentration and a heavy chest. That was a little worrying she had to concede. Beth made an appointment to see Joe and Tina, a husband and wife team of healer and psychic surgeon. She didn't talk about her belief in their abilities – no-one would believe her if she did, but she'd been to one of his courses where she learned about healing. He had built braces around her knees because he could see that the cartilages were in trouble. Indeed, Beth had been having trouble with them but hadn't told him. His healing had blown Beth away and her knees got better. For three days it felt as though she was walking a few inches above the ground. She had total belief in what Joe and Tina would find at this appointment, if there was anything to find. However, she wasn't expecting the greeting she received from them.

"Oh my goodness, come in. You look awful...so pale and drawn. Whatever is going on in your life? Go straight through and lie down as you look like you are about to collapse."

Beth wasn't aware of feeling that bad but did as she was bid and Joe was very soon at her side. He found that every one of her chakras were very, very low and in some cases almost non-existent. The heart chakra had a wobble going on which was representative of a heartbreak situation and it looked as though she was on the edge of developing uterine cancer. On those findings he decided to find out exactly why all this was happening and then came the words that explained everything. The problem she was carrying started way back at the time of Atlantis, which was a time of experimentation in the development of humanisation. Something had gone very wrong with one such experiment and Beth's soul had promised to forever look after the soul of the other. The dream of the harbour came back into her mind. Joe explained that the only way to overcome this promise was to break the bond that had been in place between the two souls for all those thousands of years – was Beth willing for him to break it? She agreed on the understanding that the other soul – Mark – would be all right. Apparently, yes, he would. All it would mean was that he would have to learn to look after himself instead of relying on her soul to do it for him. That is why Beth had been so ill, her very soul was being sucked dry albeit quite unintentionally. When she returned to her car, emotions all over the place – happy/sad, pleased/guilty, worried/relieved, and fearful/reassured. She picked up her mobile and punched out Mark's number. She spoke of all that had happened and been explained to her. When she had finished there was a deafening silence for a few seconds until, in a voice she didn't recognise from Mark, she heard him say quietly and almost, but not quite, angrily,

"I didn't want it broken."

A few seconds later the call ended and, as it turned out, they never spoke again. She missed him for a long time and hoped he would eventually come to understand. So that had been her job – to free him from her promise to look after him so that he could start to look after himself, and to free herself, of course. Although it brought great physical and emotional pain, it was what had to happen. What an experience! She went home and looked up as much about ancient Egypt as she could...and there it was...a picture of a human with a crocodile's head. That was all the verification she needed. Piece one of her life was in place. She stopped abruptly when she caught a glimpse of herself in the mirror, surprised to see that she was looking so much better. Her auburn hair had got some of its bounce back and her face had become a little softer, rounder, pinker, and her eyes...she would have to work that one out. They looked pained but relieved, if ever two such emotions could exist in the same place at the same time. Generally, she looked better than she had for a good while. Over the next few months the improvement continued and it surprised her to realise just how ill she had looked.

Beth's thoughts returned to the present and she found herself rubbing her abdomen as she did back then all those years ago when Mark had been on the scene. It was Saturday afternoon, and her friend who came in for a couple of hours to catch up with everything going on in life would be here very soon. Beth had lost touch with much going on when she started caring for her parents; now she only had one parent yet the demand for her time had seemed to double. Mother couldn't help it. She was still grieving and probably would do so for evermore.

Frankie knocked on Beth's door, let herself in and called, "Hi, Beth...it's me...got the kettle on?" She made her way to the kitchen which was, as everyone knew, the hub of every woman's home.

"Of course I have," came the happy reply.

It was almost an hour later that Frankie picked up a bundle of handwritten pages and without reading anything asked, "Getting some new ideas?"

"I thought that could be the opening two pages of the

book I'm thinking of writing. It is going to be written as fiction although most of it will be true – not that anyone would believe it," Beth said to her friend as they sat at the kitchen table, empty mugs beside them.

"What on earth do you mean? Are you following the theory that behind every legend there is some truth, or have you researched a character...like Jack the Ripper, or something?" asked Frankie.

"You and I have known each other long enough for me to talk from the hip," she said. "Let me make a sandwich for us and get the scones, cream and jam out, and a large pot of tea...and I will try to explain."

CHAPTER FOUR

There were 20 steps to go down and it looked so grey, brown, green, dank and small. The steps of a tower, built around a central pillar, steep and narrow, giving a very real feeling of foreboding and something she really didn't want to do. They were the least inviting steps you could imagine but, doing as instructed, she began to count hesitantly as she went... 1. 2. 3. 4. 5. 6. KEEP GOING... 7. 8. 9. 10. 11. 12. 12. 12. 12. 12. WHAT'S WRONG? I can't get past 13. WELL, JUMP OVER IT – MISS IT OUT...14, 15, 16..17..18..19....20 – and into an empty room. GO ON THROUGH THE DOOR. OPEN IT. Into a field of stubble and brown earth she went. Looking down, she saw dainty, bare, white feet skimming effortlessly over the stubbly earth but there was no pain. Slim ankles and lower shins showed below the hem of the heavy brown gathered skirt of her dress; the sleeves of the white under blouse clipped in at the elbow and covering the lily white beautiful arms. She saw in her mind a pretty little girl of about three years old with golden curly hair falling loosely around her shoulders – just like her own had been. The child was standing amongst tall flowers and grasses, with not a care in the world. She looked again at where she was – still in the field – but it was getting dark. She reached the caravan, a wooden, round topped one, where the man and the boy busied themselves around the small fire, waiting for the rabbit to cook. How odd. They were different to her. She was pale with golden hair; the boy, aged about 10 was black haired, and the man, a wiry little man, dressed in a green, tight and ill-fitting suit. He was a dark and shadowy character. Tinkers...they were tinkers! A picture flashed into her mind of a house, a house standing tall and large with many windows. It spoke of a wealthy family. She was sitting by the campfire now and the man moved towards her. He bent over to pick up a stone which fitted comfortably in the palm of his hand, and he struck her on the left temple. She fell over, bleeding. The man and boy hitched the horse to the caravan and went on their way. Rose was left in the field as night fell. She didn't see the morning – at 19, Rose was dead. She never got to the impressive house where she knew she had to go.

"I'M CALLING YOU BACK NOW...5, 4, 3, 2, 1...NOW OPEN YOUR EYES. Hello, how are you feeling? Would you like to talk to me about your regression?" asked the therapist.

"I was stolen as a very young child by tinkers – or I was sold to them. No, no, I was stolen. I was from a wealthy family and playing somewhere in grasses and flowers. I was stolen. I had been brought up by this tinker; he had a son about half my age. I don't know what happened to the boy's mother, she wasn't in the scene anywhere. I got the impression that I had to bring the boy up for a long period of his life. It was obvious I didn't belong with them because they were dark and swarthy looking and I was pale skinned with golden hair. There was something about a large house that I wanted to go to but the tinker hit me with a large stone. It seemed that he didn't want me to go there so he killed me. Or maybe he just meant to stun me while he and the boy made a getaway so that I could not tell anyone where they had gone. Either way, I died at 19. Why did I want to go to the house? Why was it important? Maybe I just wanted to get out of their way of life – that would fit. Yes, I must have wanted a new way of life, as I clearly didn't belong to them. What I saw was in slow motion and when he lifted his arm to hit me...her...it was no more than shoulder high and didn't appear to be a vicious swipe. How sad."

"Well, take all that away with you and you may find that more comes to you over the next few days or so. Are you OK with what we have done today?" asked the therapist as she helped Beth gather herself together before leaving.

"Yes thanks...actually, I think it answers a few things," came the reply and Beth departed with much on her mind.

"Wow," said Beth's friend, when she heard the story. "That's quite amazing. Do you think it is true? When did this happen – all of it – the tinker scene and the regression? How long have you been sitting on this?"

"The regression was probably 15 years ago," answered Beth. "And the tinker scene I feel was mid 1700s or something like that. I'm not very good on history, but that is the feeling I have. But then I had the dream to go with it which helped somewhat."

"What dream?" asked Frankie.

On her guard, Beth replied. "Ah, the dreams. I'm afraid you are going to think I am a right wacko if I tell you."

And Frankie immediately rejoined with, "I think you are a right wacko anyway, so spill."

"OK. Well, in this case I dreamt of a girl of about the same age as Rose and in the same kind of dress running down an earthen road towards a large house. Not an elaborate house but clearly the home of someone wealthy. In the doorway stood a man dressed in a pale blue brocade jacket, waistcoat and knee-length breeches, with white stockings and buckled shoes which were black, or an incredibly dark brown. He wore one of those judges' wigs. There was the softness of candlelight coming through the doorway behind him as he stood with his hands clasped behind him, a distant look on his face. What was it? Sadness?

Worry? Searching? The pain of sorrow, that's it! He was waiting for something with not much hope of it happening, I think. He looked to be about 60 years old. Anyway, she ran into the house. It looked as though she was running away from something but also into something – quite a strange feeling about it really. By the time she arrived the man was gone and the house was just one very large area. It was completely bare, no furniture, no pictures, no fireplace, nothing. And, perhaps more peculiarly, no ceiling and, therefore, no upstairs even though the house was tall enough to have an upstairs and had upstairs windows...completely empty...except for a staircase at the centre of the wall to her right. The staircase divided halfway up to go left and right but both were just cut off and went nowhere. And that was the end of the dream."

"So this dream came after your regression?" asked Frankie. "It came in afterwards as additional information?"

"Um, no. The dream was about 20-25 years ago," Beth answered, not expecting her friend to believe her.

Frankie's exclamation of 'HOW long? And you remembered it?' didn't dispel Beth's thought and she replied, "Yes. Apparently, that is one of the pointers that a dream is a real flashback – remembering them in detail and finding that all the detail is correct. I have verified the clothes, which is why I think my time frame is correct for the tinker thing."

"I am beginning to feel intrigued. Put it all together for me...you know more, don't you?" asked Frankie as she moved towards the kitchen. "I'll make another pot of tea while you start talking."

"Oh, where to start?" Beth called out to Frankie. "How much do you know of my life? I think you will have to prepare yourself to be bored to tears and hear about my upbringing. Let's clear away all these plates and stuff while I'm talking. Well, you know it was mum, dad, my brother and me, and you know that my brother and I never got on...actually, no, you sit down and read these ramblings. You read and I will clear away and make the tea. It might give you an idea of why things for me have always been...um, not quite straightforward shall we say."

Beth rubbed her abdomen as a sharp pain made itself known and then set herself about clearing away.

Frankie started to read:

Born in the house I lived in until adulthood – an old stone farm cottage, two-up two-down. It was just mum, dad, my brother and I until grandad came to live with us when I was seven. He, a stonemason by trade, did lots of renovations to the place, the first thing being to put in a bathroom and septic tank. The roof pitch was uneven, one short and one long, which meant there was a triangular box room at the back of the house. It was the full length of the house with one small window and one door. Jeez, I hated that room and would only ever go just inside the door. Grandad helped to raise the roof, so to speak, thus creating two bedrooms under a flat roof – yay...box room no more – my bedroom becoming the one where the window and door had been. If left upstairs alone I would run down the stairs and slam the door behind me (stairs had a door at the bottom). I was very young and not tall enough to reach the latch and every time dad would scream, "HOW MANY TIMES HAVE I TOLD YOU NOT TO SLAM THAT DOOR?" I couldn't tell him that there was someone chasing me, trying to push me down the stairs, when there was no-one to be seen! It was a horrible feeling – imagine someone standing so closely behind you that you can feel their body even though they aren't touching you – that's what it was like. I always felt threatened and can only assume it emanated from the end of the box room I wouldn't go into. Never found out who it was although I later learned to call it Henry. The dark and I are not good friends and we lived very rurally – no real roads, let alone street lights. In my teens I remember lying in bed hearing Morse code. Pity I didn't know Morse code! I stayed alone in that house just once – my word, never again. Nothing happened but it was some bumpy night. Perhaps Henry was there looking after me. You never know.

I think Henry probably attached himself to me when I was born and was never going to hurt me at all; maybe he just wanted me to talk to him. Much later on we looked up the records of the house at the County Records archives – who lived there, who owned it, who the tenant was, and when. It was hundreds of years old and we got back to 1754 for some information. No Henrys – a couple of vicars, but no Henrys. I grew up feeling different, odd, didn't seem to fit in anywhere and certainly not at school. The teachers hated me because of my surname, courtesy of my brother who pre-dated me at the school. He and I fought tooth and nail. My father seemed alienated and I was scared witless of him but in later years came to realise that, actually, that was my mother's doing. It was as though she...well, she is a controlling and quite jealous person and I think she has never been able to share emotions. The only person she didn't control was my brother.

Nightmares often tormented me. One, which repeated itself, was of a giant spider on my back and I suppose there is significance. I do have a phobia of spiders but did that come before or after the dream? Do spiders represent troubles, woes or something nasty I couldn't shake off in a previous life? All these dreams are written down somewhere. They all mean something. Why, for instance, am I fearful of losing my children or getting lost myself, and fearful of losing friends? Why do I not like being first or last in a queue? Right at this moment I feel like being on my own to work out where to go next, what to do next, find out what it's all about. Am I truly where I want to be, or where I am meant to be?

Frankie finished reading and saw Beth smile as she answered a text whilst making the pot of tea. She thought, "Oh, yes! Multi-tasking, that's what we women do." As Frankie put the pages down she said, "What on earth did your brother do at school to make the teachers hate you? No, tell me later. Does this fit in with the tinker thing or the running girl thing? I'm afraid I am a long way behind you."

Beth composed herself to explain. "Easy bit first. I think the running girl was the one who had been stolen by the tinkers. I also think that the man in the doorway was her biological father who waited in hope of her return but she never came. He died, never having been reunited with his daughter. Hence, when she ran into the house he was gone. The empty house represented the home she missed, and for the man it represented the home empty of his child. The staircase represented the two ways of life she had; in the end both were leading nowhere."

"What's the hard bit?" asked the interested Frankie, and she detected a well-controlled sadness within her friend as Beth measured her reply.

"My mother, in her younger days, had almost black hair, my father had fair hair, as did my brother and I. My mother seemed to put up a wall between my father and me – it was almost like he was her husband and I should not share him directly – everything had to go through her. Similarly, it seemed to be worked in reverse in that he was kept away from me, emotionally anyway. It's hard to believe now but I was always a timid child who wouldn't say boo to a goose, let alone purposely misbehave. She would never bring my brother to heel. I got to know my father later in life – in my mid-thirties onwards I suppose – and found that, actually, he was quite a nice chap. I was able to nurse him at the end of his life and held his hand as he passed. My mother always put the mockers on anything I tried to do... 'We'll see' always being the deflector which could go on for weeks until the last minute statement of 'no, it's too late for me to ask your father now'. She watched me make a dress for an end of term function and then on the day said that I couldn't go. Again she hadn't even mentioned it to dad. Decades later I concluded that she was my tinker father, and dad was the biological dad waiting in the doorway. At least in this incarnation he got me back eventually and I was there at his death. My brother? Not sure but as he always seemed to display a kind of jealousy towards me I can only assume he was the tinker brother – jealous this time round probably because I had both fathers and he had to share his with me again."

She continued. "The first thing I remember about my brother is him deliberately smashing my bottle of milk as I lay in my cot. My mother just let him slink off without telling him off. I was very young but it seems my first baby words were at 6 months old... 'dub a dee' would you believe. Apparently my mother couldn't work out that I was trying to say 'cup of tea'! What he did at school, well, let me just say he pushed the headmaster into the canal, stripped his garden of all the strawberries and laughed at him when the punishment of 'No football for you, boy' was dished out. They couldn't punish him so they decided to punish me and they did so, quite spectacularly, yet my parents did nothing. Maybe I didn't tell my mother or she wouldn't tell my father...who knows now?"

"So what makes you think that Rose was you...is you...you are her?" asked Frankie, with the question written all over her face.

Reaching for a scone Beth replied, "There are a few things which have come to my notice when I wasn't looking for them. For instance, at 19 I had an ovarian cyst removed by surgery. Without that surgery I would have died. Rose died at 19 – loose connection I know, but it is there. I was always cold in general but especially in my feet and about four inches above the ankles. Brown – I have never worn brown and never will – it is a colour I just do not like. I have no sense of direction and I'm always afraid of getting lost. My sight is poorest in my left eye and always has been. Have never wanted to go camping and can't ever envisage a time when I would want to. However, I do love looking at the stars."

Frankie read again the opening pages of the proposed story, drew in a breath in readiness to say something, then looked at her friend as if a realisation had hit home. Eventually she falteringly asked, "Sunday 31 March 2013 – that was the day your dad died, wasn't it? I...we... everyone was amazed at the change in you after that day; a calmness seemed to wrap itself around you. We thought you'd have been in pieces, found it difficult to get over his awful illness, not to mention the strain of looking after your mother at the same time as him. Them both being nonagenarians did not make it very easy. I'll never understand how you coped... is this true? Is it real, I mean, it doesn't sound very...how does this work? How did you know? How?"

With the arrival of a little confidence Beth began,"The thing is, I really feel as if I've been gifted my past. Oh, I'm not explaining myself very well...um, have you thought about what you really believe in? What keeps you going through life? What do you hold on to when things get difficult?"

Frankie's eyes drifted in pursuit of an answer. "I..., I think I more or less try to see the problem and do what I can to sort it out and if I can't then, well... you've seen the results...not always pretty. I haven't got any strong religious beliefs if that is what you mean," she said looking a little bewildered.

"No, I don't mean religion. I can't say I have any strong religious beliefs either – well, yes, I suppose I have, but from a bit of a different angle. Look, are you free tomorrow after 6pm? Come with me – I'll pick you up," offered Beth.

"You think it will help me to understand all this in your story?"

"I think it will help a bit, yes. We are going to church. Jeans and jumper, no ceremony."

Beth was suddenly interrupted by a panic stricken friend saying, "Sing – have I got to sing? I don't do singing."

Laughing Beth answered, "Pick a note, any note, and pitch it where you want...or you can mime if you want."

Frankie headed for home, not quite sure what that meant but smiled at the thought that she could mime if she wanted to. That was reassuring.

Beth picked up her mobile phone:

Write message: "Frankie has just gone. Boy, did we talk. And I had the nerve to ask if YOU had more to say after Thursday...! B." Press send.

Buzz buzz. "I can't complain at that. Have just been chatting to Hazel. J"

Write message: "That's OK, then. B"

Hazel worked at the village shop. She was a busybody type of person who liked to put her twopenn'orth into everyone else's business as if she was trying to control the outcome for them. Beth had always got on with her all right, never had cause to argue or get cross with her, but she also had no inclination to become friends. There was something about her that did not lend her to becoming a friend. Acquaintance, yes...friend, no. When Beth thought about it she realised it was obviously just one of those things when you know instinctively on meeting someone whether you are going to like them or not. Hazel had never given her any reason to dislike her, but there was something there that didn't endear her to Beth either. Just one of those things.

CHAPTER FIVE

Beth and Frankie walked into the Spiritualist Church, which, much to the surprise of Frankie, was more like walking into a party. No-one was sitting primly and properly, and there was a cacophony of voices and laughter from a bunch of people genuinely pleased to see one another. A lady turned, beamed at them both and walked towards them, arms outstretched.

"Hello dear, how are you today? Mother behaving? How's your daughter getting on?" Then she turned to Frankie, put her hand on her arm and said, "Hello, dear – is this your first visit? Come on in – this is Alison, Lavinia, Naomi, James, Jo and I'm Anne – oh, and this is Malcolm. Hope you enjoy the service."

Already bemused and amused, Frankie began to indulge in thoughts of how the evening would unfold. No vicar it seemed, but a speaker. Hmm. The service was due to start in five minutes – where was the pianist? The hymn numbers were not on the board; in fact, there wasn't a board, yet everyone was clutching a hymn book. Oh no!

Unaccompanied singing – pick a note... a hush descended. Malcolm looked at his watch and all eyes turned to the door. A moment later it burst open and a lady of about 70, dyed black hair and rusty-red lipstick, all but fell through the doorway. Her left hand clasped a hat to her head, with a small suitcase clutched under the other arm. She had the biggest contagious grin on her face.

"Oh dear, sorry," she said, her foot automatically going out behind her to close the door. She bustled her way through the throng, twisting this way and that, giving a greeting to everyone to her left and right on the way, sometimes doing a full circle to do so. Quite out of breath she reached the piano and the suitcase, which Frankie had noticed slipping lower and lower every time this wonderful character turned, finally fell to the floor spilling its contents of sheet music and books, the lady still proclaiming, "Oh dear, sorry."

She began haphazardly gathering it all together, a finer mess Frankie had never seen. This did Frankie no good at all, failing superbly at disguising giggles. Then, there it was, the one brief moment where this strange woman took an intake of breath.

"Hello Joan," came a chorus. "What have you got for us tonight?"

Without stopping Joan began again, still scrabbling on the floor at all that music – the energy, where on earth did she get the energy?

"Let's see, I thought maybe..." and she quickly looked at a sheet and put it down again. "Or...it's here somewhere...no...oh! What about this? Let's have this one first – yes, here we go..."

By which time somehow she had got herself sat at the piano and began playing.

"Joan...Joan... JOAN..." it was Malcolm's voice.

"Yes, dear? No good?"

"It's fine Joan. What is it? We ought to know which words to sing," he said, looking awfully innocent.

Joan again fumbled with the music, "Oh, yes...it's...here we are...Let All the World In Every Corner Sing...number...no, no...yes, 537." And she began playing the introduction again.

"Number 357," announced Malcolm, but they were both wrong...it was number 375.

And off they went, just as Beth had said, with many different voices and tones. Joan, she discovered, wasn't singing the wrong tune but sang alto notes to everything, something she had always done during her long career as a choir mistress. Some of the men pitched where they could and there were one or two people who were probably tone deaf. And then there was the lady at the front, clearly very proud of her ridiculously high-pitched voice. Strangely, and suddenly, Frankie felt at home. It didn't matter one little bit...they all enjoyed themselves; no right, no wrong; just enjoyment of singing – whatever it was supposed to sound like.

The speaker stood, asking everyone to find their own quiet space within and join him in thought as he said his opening prayer. Frankie had never heard anything quite so moving, so real, so...natural...and when he read out the names from the healing book she felt really quite small. All those people who needed to be held in prayer and thought because of illness or troubles of some kind, names she knew and yet didn't know they were suffering. She started thinking for herself. Then she began 'people reading' as she called it, looking at people and seeing the personality behind the person she could see. Jo...now there was a challenge. Something was not as it seemed. There was no disputing that Jo was a lovely, gentle, caring and apparently outgoing lady, but there was some sort of storm going on underneath all the laughter and smiles she gave. She had the appearance of a swan on the water, serenely gliding along the surface but feet paddling like mad underneath to keep her afloat, evidenced, Frankie decided, by the way Jo would answer like an excitable terrier.

"Yes, yes...yes, yes...oh, yes, definitely...yes," her thick, curly, blonde hair bouncing as she unconsciously nodded her head at the same time.

Frankie chided herself for thinking anything other than pure sympathetic thoughts. An excitable terrier, indeed! Poor Jo, there was obviously something this dear lady was trying to overcome. As she cast her eyes around during what replaced a traditional sermon she noticed James looking at Beth. In fact, whenever her glance crossed his way, he seemed to be looking at Beth. A sideways glance at her friend showed a very easy smile on her face.

"Hmmm," thought Frankie. "Note to me...ask about James."

On the way home she took her chance.

"I noticed James looking at you quite a lot," she asked with a cheeky grin. "Got something to tell me?"

"No, don't be daft. We get on very well and he reads music, which is how I met him on 24 March 2013."

"That's a bit precise for it to be nothing," enquired Frankie.

"Ah, I only remember it so clearly because it was the week before dad died. Joan was poorly, getting over a bit of surgery, and I'd been asked to play instead. Dad had been so ill that I'd ended up being awake for a continuous 60 hours during the week...inevitable, I suppose, that a migraine hit me on the Friday and was still lurking on Sunday. The last hymn was just too much for me. James's was the only face I didn't recognise and Anne had said there was a musician called James who had started coming to the church, so I just asked if he would be able to play as I felt so rough. He did, thankfully. He's an amazing pianist Frankie. I went to sit with him afterwards to thank him properly and then I began to shake; it was like a huge whack on the shoulder which sent shockwaves all the way down through my body, and it kept on happening; each wave coming faster on the heels of the previous one. James put his hand on my back – he's a healer, by the way; you know about healing, don't you? Yes, of course you do – and after a while it began to subside. Well, then dad died the following week and about three weeks after that Anne invited me to coffee at the garden centre. I thought it was to be just her and me but when I got there the whole group you met tonight was there, including James. I sat beside him – NO, before you ask – it just happened to be the only chair left, and we found we got on very well. We had to laugh...he said he had found it amusing afterwards that there we were in the church, him with his hand all over my back, me shaking like a rippling jelly, when I offered my hand and said, 'Hello...I'm Beth Channing...I'm very pleased to meet you.' There, now you know all about James."

"You seem to be quite animated when you talk about him, are you sure there is nothing you want to tell me?" asked Frankie hopefully.

"Do I? No, there's nothing to tell. He's just a lovely guy – gives lovely hugs, and this I only know because some of us manage to go for coffee once a week at the garden centre, and James usually says goodbye to us all with a hug," she said with a hint of a smile dancing on her face.

"Doesn't James work?" asked Frankie.

"Yes, but not full-time yet so he's taking the chance to find out more about the area and local life – he's not been here that long. I'm sure it is these weekly coffee jaunts that have been my salvation after dad. In fact, it probably helps James, too. He lost his wife in that dreadful train accident two or three years ago."

"Yes, you could be right there," said Frankie.

As they pulled up at Frankie's house Beth's mobile buzzed. She pulled it out and smiled as she looked at the message, then put it away saying, "That was James saying it was nice to see us tonight." She let the sentence trail.

"And that makes you smile, does it?" teased Frankie.

Beth looked surprised and asked, "Smile? I'm not smiling...oh, I am, aren't I?"

With an outburst of laughter Frankie said, "You bet you are, girlie." Frankie simply raised one eyebrow and continued, "It's nice to see you looking so relaxed. Thanks for the lift home. I enjoyed this evening; thank you so much for introducing me to your friends at church. The people who got messages seemed to be pleased. Are they real – the messages, I mean?"

"Very. Remember the message that Mr. Taylor had? Well, that was all about his sister. She did have an abusive husband and she did drown, and she looked exactly as described by the speaker, even down to the wonky teeth," answered Beth. "And the message I had...that was about mum's next-door neighbour. She has problems with her children – they are at various stages of education – GCSEs, uni, college. One of them doesn't know which way to go, but then you heard the message. It was absolutely correct."

Frankie lowered her head briefly, lifted it high again and said, "I have a lot to think about, haven't I?"

"Give me a shout if you want to ask any questions; if I can't help you then I'm sure Lavinia, Anne, Malcolm, Alison...any of the people you met tonight... will be happy to do so," answered Beth gently. "Good night, Frankie, I'll see you on Saturday?"

"Probably with a long list of questions," answered Frankie as she closed the car door and walked towards her house.

CHAPTER SIX

Buzz buzz. The sound of a text arriving was welcome as she was more than ready to do something different.

It read: "Hello dear, do you fancy coffee at the garden centre – the usual crowd but Malcolm is leaving early today and Alison may not be there – 11:30 OK?"

"Too right," went the reply. "See you there."

Beth was sorting her mother out for the day and it sometimes left her feeling wrung out and at a complete loss as to what to do right for her. Today was one of those days. It wasn't easy for her mother, widowed just a few months ago at the age of 92; they'd been married for 65 years. Beth's face was completely transformed by a big grin as she remembered the times she had arrived in the morning and her father would greet her, eyes popping, declaring, "Hello, maid. I can't take this much longer, I'm ready to walk; I don't know what's wrong with your mother – she's in a proper mood again today. It isn't easy living with her, you know; I can't take it much longer..."

To which she always replied, "Oh dear. I'll go and find her and see if I can get any sense out of her. You start walking, don't forget your stick, and I'll catch you up in a minute."

That always made him laugh and the seriousness of the moment diffused into the air. He meant it; he always meant it. Her mother could, indeed, be a difficult character. He even threatened to take his mobility scooter, saying, "I can get plenty far enough away...8 miles an hour is fast enough to outrun her."

With his face still in her mind she finished her jobs and left for coffee with her friends.

They all sat around the table as usual with Alison to Beth's right, then Jo, Anne, Lavinia, Malcolm and, coming back full circle, with James to her left. She answered all questions about Frankie so, eventually, the bunch of friends had a potted history of her...that she was widowed ten years ago and moved to the next village a year or two after that and it was one of those purely accidental meetings that began their friendship. If Frankie hadn't gone into Marks & Spencer's changing rooms at that time she would not have heard Beth huffing and puffing and sounding quite distraught. Being the friendly bod that Frankie was, she spoke through the curtain only to be welcomed in by legs and arms flailing around as whoever was inside the dress was desperately trying to get out of it. After a bit of an organised tussle the 5ft 7in bundle of Beth popped out of the offensively small garment and a new friendship was forged.

As the laughter subsided the conversation rolled into each of their personal histories; Malcolm, being not far off retirement age, had taken voluntary redundancy and was thoroughly enjoying life with his wife, Jackie. They had a beautiful camper van and managed to get away as and when they wanted. He had worked in the council's planning department and his wife had been a special needs teacher. James got on very well with Jackie and Malcolm; teaching was a much discussed subject between them. Lavinia was the eldest of them and had long been retired from the health profession. The injuries her father sustained in the war sparked an interest that led to her becoming a nurse, later specialising in mental health. Apart from taking time to raise her family, she had worked until 'put out to grass', as she put it, and then took on childcare duties for her grandchildren. Now, at 80, she was trying to slow down a little but she had to admit, with her beautifully soft chuckle, that she 'was failing amazingly well so far'. Anne had also been a nurse but was happy to remain an SEN and combine it with raising the family she and Tom were so proud of. Now she was fully trained in reflexology, Reiki, Qi Gong and was currently studying herbalism. Her husband was happily and newly retired, spending as much time as possible with his train set in the shed. Jo, at 45, was the youngest and worked as a stress, anxiety and depression counsellor. It was ironic – the poor lady was on sick leave due to precisely that – stress and depression. She had never married but had quite a large family dotted up and down the country. Alison had worked at a care home before she and her accountant husband, Bernie, retired. Being together all the time was now driving her quite mad and she was always ready for the coffee morning get-togethers. They had two sons who both lived abroad. Beth looked at her own life – left to bring up her children more or less alone, not because she was husbandless but because Michael worked permanent nights and was never around. That was why, when he did leave her for someone else, she didn't find it particularly difficult or stressful. Life just seemed to continue much as usual. He carried on seeing the children, visiting as and when he wanted – or they wanted him to – and was still a frequent visitor to the house. It had all been very civilised. What was the point of it being anything else? She thought back to the Down's syndrome baby they had elected to terminate. They both realised that this was a tough but correct decision, especially as they already had a son suffering with asthma, which had already tried to claim him twice, stress being a trigger. To bring extra difficulties into their family could possibly see them lose both Daniel and the second child. Many Down's babies do not survive the first year of life. What a decision to have to make; one of, if not THE, worst times of her life. But life goes on, as the adage goes. Now she was happy being single and very happy to see her children slide into adulthood and fly with their own lives. She looked at the group as a whole – nurses, carers and teachers, most with a problem of some sort – what a wonderful bunch they were. No wonder they all got on so well together.

CHAPTER SEVEN

The man sprawled at the feet of the emperor, or someone who looked every inch an emperor, was desperately looking for someone to help him, begging for his life. Dressed in loose, beige trousers cut off just below the knees and an equally loose, simply cut top, his narrow, lined face was contorted with fear. He made a truly pitiful sight. The emperor stood before him, unmoved, his green and yellow silk robes, sleeves lined with red, resplendent and dripping with wealth and power. The little black hat on his dark hair and the Fu Manchu style facial hair completed this rather fearsome picture. Against the wall was a large table absolutely covered by cylindrical bottles of various sizes – some full, some not. This poor man, was he a physician? His clothes spoke more of a lowly worker, maybe a paddy field worker. Whoever he was, his life was not spared. What on earth had he done to lose his life in this way? The answer to that was not given in the dream but, unusually, a name was. Xiang. Even more unusually, Beth's own thoughts found their way through and she said to the emperor, "I promise to be the best healer I possibly can." He then looked directly at Beth as she observed the scene of the dream and gave an almost imperceptible nod.

It was Saturday afternoon again and Frankie read the story of the Chinese man but said nothing for a moment or two. "This was another dream?" she finally asked. "But what makes you think this is relevant to past life stuff? You do think it is past life stuff, like Rose?"

Beth showed her some paperwork. "Yes. This one, I think goes back maybe as far as BC years..." she began.

"You're kidding!" exclaimed Frankie.

Beth pulled a few pieces of paper from her folder saying, as she passed them to Frankie, "That name Xiang, which was even spelled out for me, captured my interest so I went on to Google to see what I could find out. Have a read of it and see what you make of it."

Frankie soon became engrossed as she read:

Xiang Xiang!! What century? BC I think. Emperor?

Via Google found possibilities for BC and AD.

Place: Xiang – a county-level city in Xiangton in Huron Province.

Yangtze River (Chang Jiang)... Xiang Xiang???

Relics from Daxi culture indicates Xiangton inhabited in the 3rd millennium BC.

SHANG dynasty bronze wares found and tombs from Warring States Period.

During Three Kingdoms Period, Kingdom of Eastern Wu built a city west of modern Xiangton City and organised the Hengyang commanders around it. In AD749 the Tang Dynasty organised the area as Xiangton County, centred at modern Yisu River. By Northern Song Dynasty Xiangton's good access to land and water trade routes had established it as the major commercial centre of the region. Xiangton prospered throughout the Ming and Qing Dynasties upon an economic foundation of trading in rice and traditional Chinese medicinal ingredients and sometimes regarded as "Little Nanjing" or "Golden Xiangton." Before second opium war Xiangton was central transfer point for import/export goods to/from Canton, Shanghai and Wuhan.

Daxi sites typified by presence of DOU – cylindrical bottles! White pan (plates) and red pottery. Daxi people cultivated rice extensively. Daxi culture: 5,000 – 3,000BC. Modern day location – Three Gorges Region. A picture on Google of Three Gorges shows 2 mountains and water in front (Three Gorges Dam). Three Gorges region has many settlements and archaeological sites under submersion from the rising Three Gorges Dam. (MY MEDITATION VISION COMES TO MIND HERE – 2 mountains with treetops!)

I think this was the time of the Yellow King and the Fire King (Red)…eventually brought together to create the modern day Han people of China. Around 5,000 years ago Lei Su, wife of the Yellow Emperor, discovered silk – produced first garments – ancient people then bid goodbye to wearing skins and leaves. Xiang Dynasty 4,000 years ago. China entered period of slave society. Shang Dynasty (16th-11th centuries BC) height of bronze culture. Beautiful bronze wares and pottery developed. Sericulture and silk weaving reached maturity at this time.

In my dream, Xiang (if that was his name) was the top dog. The gown was the real McCoy. Pillbox type of hat (interesting). Fu Manchu moustache, hair and beard. Gown was yellow with green trim and red inside the large sleeves. Could this be a reference to the Yellow Emperor and Fire (Red) Emperor? "My" emperor had the rounded face of a Mongolian and looked fearsome. Who was the poor man begging for his life? Healer or doctor? Large table completely covered in cylindrical bottles – assumed to be medicines. Is this a reference to the Daxi sites? Message was clear...he had done his best but something had gone wrong so he was executed.

Something about the emperor in my dream made me think of the emperor in the Disney film "Mulan" so was this so I would know he was an emperor or was it to help with the possible year? The ballad of Mulan was first transcribed in the 6th century...the one before the founding of Tang Dynasty. Original writing was way b4 then...Xu Wei's play version places her of Northern Wei Dynasty 386-536. Mulan's father described in both as stemming from people of Northern Wei.

Ballad of Mulan...

Her name: Mulan – History of Ming = Zhu; History of Qing = Wei.

Family name, Hua, was introduced by Xu Wei and it was accepted as being more poetic.

Xiang Wang Zheng 651-619BC was King Xiang of Zhou.

Zhou Dynasty 690-705...NB 2 me, double check this.

Zheng = forename, Xiang Wang = surname.

Was 18th king of Zhou Dynasty.

"So this man could actually have been a rice grower and maybe his rice had been contaminated, or perhaps he hadn't grown enough? I just don't know and possibly never will. If I am supposed to know it will be given to me one day, but I really do think there is a past life thing going on here. Listen to this other dream," Beth said as Frankie rested her chin on her hand and started to listen intently. "Do you remember I told you about the Down's syndrome baby? Well, years ago I dreamt of a Down's child aged 10. Don't ask me how I knew he was 10, it's just one of those things that I know when I'm dreaming. Plus Daniel was in the dream at the age he really was. It all worked right with the ages, anyway. Also the baby was due to be born on the 23rd May 1990 and I dreamt this on the 24th May 2000. In the dream this 10-year-old child walked down my stairs, happy and grinning but very much a Down's child. Daniel was right behind him, quite unperturbed and said, "Look who I've found in my room, mum.""

I gently said to the Down's child. "I'm so sorry, but you can't stay." I've always thought of him as Adam by the way – the baby was definitely a boy. Then the dream started all over again with them both coming down the stairs and my son saying, "Look who I found in my room again." Both of them were smiling. Again I gently said to Adam, "I'm so terribly sorry, you know you can't stay but, before you go, can you please show me how you got in?" He showed me a key, and then the dream ended completely.

"OK," said Frankie. "Explain."

Beth dunked a biscuit, took a couple of mouthfuls of tea and began. "I think the obvious connection is Down's syndrome, or Mongolism, as it was once referred to. The emperor looked Mongolian and the man begging for his life looked more Chinese. In fact, now I think about it, I believe Mongolia invaded China and took their Master Craftsmen at some stage in history, so it is possible that the Chinese man begging for his life was a physician of that time. Whatever it really is, I think the emperor wrongly took the man's life and it has taken this long for him to be able to atone for that deed. This time, although it is a past life thing, I believe this one only involves me rather than directly linking to my soul. I suspect that the man whose life was taken was actually Daniel's soul. The more I dwell on it, the more likely it seems that it took the emperor this long to right a dreadful wrong because the soul of the unfortunate man found it impossible to forgive, thereby prohibiting any chance of it happening. I think the emperor's soul came into my second baby, knowing that Daniel's life would again be seriously compromised if Adam was born. The emperor's soul made me feel so poorly myself that the decision to terminate would perhaps be a little easier to bear. I firmly believe the emperor gave his own life so that Daniel could live in this lifetime, and the only way he could do it was to involve me."

Frankie sat upright and quietly asked, "And the key in the dream represents Daniel? It all came in because of Daniel? What do your friends at church think of this? You've told them about it, yes?"

Beth looked out of the window at the nurses going into the house almost directly opposite and thought about her neighbour – she should never be living alone, she needed specialist care. Alcoholism had been her downfall and it had now affected her mind as well. At only 68 she looked more like 88 – unkempt, shuffling, reclusive. Bringing her mind back to the kitchen and the mug in her hand she quietly admitted, "I've not actually told anyone else about this; not sure why."

Frankie thought for a moment and then, with a serious tone, asked, "Why did you choose me?"

"Because neither of us mind if you tell me I am a raving lunatic!" Beth said with a laugh, which had the desired effect of breaking the seriousness of the situation.

"Well then," said Frankie. "Is there any more to tell me before I finally make up my mind on that?"

"Lots, and if I tell it all to you now you will have me certified within a week!" joked Beth. "There are the rest of the dreams, and the 'other' dreams."

Frankie looked at her with questioning eyes and answered, "I shall look forward to hearing about them."

This was not the time to pursue it. Beth brought the subject to a close as she said, "Shall we have some of this pavlova and another cup of tea before Michael arrives?"

CHAPTER EIGHT

Michael was still her husband; he had never wanted to marry Pauline, the woman he'd spent the past 14 years with, and Beth hadn't met anyone. Life had just rolled along and everything stayed the same but in a different way, as the saying went. He was coming over that night to catch up with news of the children. They weren't children any more, of course. Daniel was married himself now and living 40 miles away. A thought popped in to Beth's mind – ha! Emily was another nurse – all these nurses in her life! They were too young to get married Michael had said but he finally gave his blessing. Charlotte was having a bit of a holiday before starting at the University of Southampton in September. Getting his approval for that was another struggle. Why on earth did everything have to be a struggle with him when, in the end, he always admitted that he didn't have a problem with any of it? It was as though he just had to make things difficult for the fun of it. More than once Beth had likened his behaviour to that of his mother who would happily and rather proudly announce that she would, in her own words, 'argue that black was white if it suits me.'

Michael was always punctual, that much had to be said. He wasn't purposely unkind but he could deliver stunning put-downs disguised as humour – well, no – he could never see the hurtful impact that some of his brand of humour could, and did, have. He wasn't abusive in any other way. They had been through a lot together but they had drifted apart. Pure and simple, they had drifted apart. There was no passion between them and hadn't been for a few years before he left Beth for Pauline. They were friendly to one another, more or less. It was only when he decided to put up barriers that things became sticky.

"Come in," she said, walking back into the kitchen.

"Hello, Beth, nice to see you. How is Charlotte getting on in Canada? Can I put the kettle on?" he asked. "Who is she staying with at the moment?"

Beth picked up her iPad and sat at the table while Michael made the tea. "Why don't you get yourself one of these?" she asked him. "They are wonderful. You could keep up with the kids at the touch of a button. You could FaceTime them or message them...it didn't take me too long to get the hang of it. You would pick it up." She knew she was talking to deaf ears. If he had an iPad he wouldn't have so much of an excuse to come to see her and Charlotte when she was home. "With Charlotte going away to uni in September she won't be here for you to see so, you know, FaceTime would be brilliant contact for you, and you wouldn't have to keep driving all the way over here just to get second-hand news. She's staying with my cousin, Dorothy. She'll be back home soon."

"I thought your cousin lived in Germany," Michael asked absently.

"Wrong cousin – that's Erica," answered Beth, a little tersely. He knew that. Why was he being a prat?

Buzz buzz. "Excuse me a moment," Beth said as she found the message on her mobile. She smiled, and put the phone away.

"What's made you smile?" asked Michael.

"Nothing," she answered, perhaps a little too quickly for Michael's comfort. "Just a friend of mine asking if I'd like to go for a walk tomorrow afternoon." This would not be enough to satisfy Michael and, as she knew the interrogation by stealth thing could start at any time, she said it was Alison who had texted. She certainly was not going to tell him it was James.

That night as Beth lay in bed waiting for sleep to come she was surprised to find herself thinking about James, realising she was looking forward to their walk the next day. So much so, in fact, that she wanted nothing and no-one to stop it. Thank goodness Michael had made his visit that evening but what he'd said had left her unusually fretful. What was it he had said? How had he put it? "I don't think Pauline's too happy with me at the moment – must be that time of life thing you women get." Ever the understanding male she thought. What else had he said – oh yes! "We were always good together, weren't we? We didn't argue." Sure enough they hadn't argued; he'd never been around long enough for arguments. But the most unnerving thing was the quiet way he'd asked if she ever wondered what it would be like if they were still together. Gods! He couldn't be thinking of coming back. Surely not! NO, NO, NO! screamed her head as she thought again of the promised walk with her friend who was easy to talk with, debate with and laugh with. That was something which had long been missing from her life and it was about time it returned. It made her feel alive...yes, alive. Round and round her thoughts went. Only one thing for it now; a cup of chocolate Horlicks, or Snorlicks as Charlotte liked to call it. It never failed to work, this night being no exception.

The morning and Sunday lunch with her mother seemed to be longer than any other day – as Sundays often were – and her mother was weepy again and, as usual, not making too much sense. "I don't like Sundays," she'd say. "Your father died today."

Beth always replied, "Yes, mum, he did die on a Sunday, within the first hour, didn't he but, you know, he wouldn't want you sitting here like this moping. Why not come out into the garden?"

"Don't want to," mother retorted abruptly.

"Or sit in the other chair and watch the birds feeding – you like to see the birds," Beth would counter.

Today it was "No! I'd see the blasted woodpecker."

Beth knew this was the tantrum kind of reply she would not be able to get past. The woodpecker had been dad's favourite bird; no, that wasn't true. All birds were his favourite apart from magpies and pigeons, as they would plunder other birds' nests and eat all his cabbage plants in the garden respectively. No matter how she tried today there would be no getting through this one and, sadly, she realised she'd have to cancel her walk with James. In fact, this was not the first time she'd have to cancel an arrangement because of a 'tantrum'. It crossed her mind that mother knew instinctively that if she didn't throw a spanner in the works then Beth would be out having a good time while she wasn't.

She took out her mobile and punched out: "Sorry James. Can't make this afternoon as mother in a dark place today. I don't suppose you'd like to come over to my place this evening and watch a DVD with me? I've got War Horse in mind or, if that's too heavy, what about Disney's Hercules or Men in Black I or II? Sorry. B"

It wasn't long before the reply arrived. "No problem. Yes, I'd love to watch a DVD with you. War Horse is no good on your own and the other two are good to share laughter over. What time? J"

"How about 6pm? Don't eat; I've plenty of food to use up. Living alone leaves you prone to that, doesn't it? B"

As soon as she pressed the 'send' button she could have chopped her hand off. 'Living alone!' Of all the things she could have said she chose that phrase. IDIOT! She would apologise to him when he arrived.

Luckily Mrs. Taylor came to visit mother as usual in time to watch Songs of Praise and then they would 'put the world to rights' as dad always used to say. His euphemism for gossip. Still, it made mother happy for a while and tomorrow she would have something to talk about, if she could remember.

Buzz buzz. "Sorry B. Going to be a little late. Be there by 6.30pm latest. J"

No surprises thought Beth. He was often later than everyone else at church, or at the garden centre. It was just one of his things, but everyone knew so it didn't matter. If it was important James would be told an earlier time; that tended to sort it out. Not to worry, that gave her a little more time to dry her hair properly and reapply her make-up. Why? What was she doing that for? It's good to look nice for guests, she told herself. And that was right.

True to his word, James rang the doorbell before 6:30pm and it was not really surprising to Beth that she felt nervous at his arrival. She was still fretting about the possible effect of what she had said in her text and answered the door not quite sure how things would go.

"Hello," said James. "You look nice. Thank you for inviting me over; it didn't take long to find you. I hope you like red wine." He handed her a bottle.

"I'm sorry about the 'living alone' comment," she blurted out. "I know you miss your wife dreadfully. Thank you, yes, red is lovely."

He followed her into the kitchen to find a table laden with simple and beautifully presented food. "Yes, I do," he replied. "It's the not having had time to prepare myself or to say goodbye properly. I wasn't home the day it...it...um...happened so she didn't get to hear me say, 'Have a good day at work, I love you' and I didn't get to see her face one more time, and I...I'm..."

"Finding it too hard to deal with?" Beth finished for him.

James was still looking at his clasped hands as he whispered his answer "Yes."

Beth had no reply ready for that but found herself talking anyway, "I'm so sorry. I'm OK to listen if you want to talk about the accident, or your wife. People say I'm fairly good at listening, not that blowing one's trumpet is any recommendation."

"Oh, it's highly recommended," James grinned. "You should never let anyone else blow your trumpet – very unhygienic," his American twang now evident.

Her unplanned words had lifted him more than she could know; they both laughed out loud, cracked open the red wine and danced around the lounge as they listened to André Rieu playing a Strauss waltz. The evening was going to be fine.

Her sleep was short but pleasingly deep and she woke with very mixed thoughts. The first of which was of the precious time spent with James the night before and the Strauss music, how he had given her several hugs as they shared the emotion of various conversations, especially that last hug as he left her in the very early morning hours. It was so deep, so lingering, so tight yet so gentle. Then came the 'Goodnight Beth,' and his gaze held hers for a moment longer. Then he was gone leaving Beth feeling...feeling...feeling...like a grown-up teenager. That shifted her thoughts to when she was a teenager, her relationship with her father sadly lacking in just about everything. How grateful she was that she'd been shown who her dad was in a previous life and that she'd been able to reconcile their souls. It was a feeling totally indescribable in either words or action. In her heart, however, it was pure joy and filled her with a love that would be difficult for anyone who did not believe in reincarnation and everything she was experiencing in this lifetime to understand. It gave her relief, love, ease and, it pained her to think, a smugness of mind that there is a utopia where everything works out well. Then she snapped back to the reality of the moment. Yes, that situation had eventually worked out but how much pain had been suffered by how many people along the way? She thought about it. The tiny girl stolen by the tinkers – how alone, scared, ripped apart she must have felt. And what of her parents? Beth imagined all the feelings she'd have experienced if Daniel or Charlotte had disappeared without trace at such a young age – any age! That was something no parent could ever get over. She thought of the self blame, the insurmountable sorrow and the cutting hurt. No heart could ever recover from something like that. Rose's father must have blamed himself for the rest of his life. No doubt he had done everything humanly possible to find her, employed people to search, yet she remained out of his reach. And all the while Rose knowing that she didn't belong to her 'family' of tinkers, yet probably never remembering where she truly belonged. The emptiness of the hearts of both the girl and her father tore Beth to shreds. Then came a moment of realisation which added yet more credence to her belief. Her own father had suffered impatience for as long as she could remember. He suffered from high blood pressure for almost as long and, in the last 30 years, heart failure culminating in a small stroke. It was the cancer that finally claimed him, but all the other things were symptomatic of a man whose heart was breaking. She rubbed her abdomen until it felt comfortable again.

She considered how this was part of the reincarnation process. When the pain is so great the soul keeps going until it can in some way put right whatever wrong may have occurred. In Beth's case it had culminated in a replay of Rose's life, with different scenery. All those souls had come together again – the tinker and his son, her biological father and herself – to play out some kind of spiritual battle. The tinker's soul wanting to win again, the biological father's soul hanging on in there quietly waiting for his daughter's soul to recognise him, the brother's soul? Well, it looked as though he was resolutely taking the side of his father who, of course, was their mother in this incarnation, his soul clearly viewing their dad's soul as the one now trying to steal her from them. His open displays of jealousy were his way of kicking against everything – the establishment, convention, families – he was staying as apparently unscrupulous as the life of a tinker seemed to dictate. Whether by choice or by birth a tinker's life then was spent fighting for survival by whatever means there was. If it meant stealing, which it invariably did, then they stole. How else were they to survive unless they travelled the land taking any work an itinerant could get? Not a guaranteed way of life. Lord knows life these days could be hard even with the huge and very varied benefits system now in place for those on low incomes, out of work, disabled and so on. Many still lived on the streets in cardboard boxes and all because of some terrible disaster in their life. There was one local character who fell outside of this category; Jim, an erudite man who, many years ago, had simply walked out of everyday life and taken to the road in his horse-drawn caravan with a dog for company. Everyone knew and loved 'Traveller Jim' and looked forward to the days when his travels brought him back to their area. Thankfully, Beth thought, her own and her father's soul had managed FINALLY to reconcile their connection so cruelly torn apart all those centuries ago. That, of course, now left her mother's and brother's souls to deal with their sides of the story although, she realised, maybe a lot was for her to sort out for them as they were not going to see it for themselves. Perhaps they simply weren't ready, or maybe because both had jealous streaks it would never happen.

'There's none so blind as those who will not see,' she recalled her grandmother saying so many times and she wondered if her lovely granny was trying to warn her of mother's nature. Both she and her brother readily decried Beth's spiritual beliefs, openly displaying their total unwillingness to recognise how everyone has a past that has an effect on their present. Until they could accept that, there was no chance at all of them putting it to rest. All her own efforts to make them see that she was not a threat to them in any way and that she loved them for who they were was clearly failing. Perhaps she could let this go now, once and for all, and leave them to live with their elements of retribution for past actions. Mother would have to stay controlling and her brother would continue being jealous. Beth would have to carry on glossing over it but she didn't need to let them think it was perfectly all right to treat her in such a way of course. She had become quite adept at finding suitable phrases to make them both see what they were doing, but it changed nothing. It was a small price for her to pay for being able to find her old dad again, let him know she was home and that he'd remained in her heart all these past centuries.

The morning with her mother had been lovely. Mother was happy and everything was right in her world, something Beth had not seen too much of since her dad had died. Sometimes she thought that mother was using that as an excuse to be miserable; it was hard to tell if she really was suffering some kind of early dementia, or if it was more of an attention-seeking exercise. Alison had worked in care homes for many years and had met all kinds of behaviours along the way. She was very good indeed at working out if a person's behaviour was due to dementia or not. With Beth's mother, however, Alison could not form an opinion easily, but she was more inclined to think that it was a case of attention-seeking. Well, it looked as if Alison may be correct – Alan and Cathy Townsend were calling on her today. Alan had been dad's apprentice in the past. So long ago it didn't bear thinking about, though he had maintained contact when dad retired 30 years ago. Alan himself was newly retired and was continuing the visits to Beth's mother. And how grateful Beth was. She went to the shop to get a cake and some biscuits for mum to offer with tea and coffee, where Hazel seemed to make a beeline for her and asked her how the evening had gone with James. Beth was going to give nothing away, especially to Hazel who was regarded as someone who may not be able to keep things to herself. Hazel tried to drag it out of Beth by saying what a nice chap she thought James was and began asking several questions. Not to be drawn into conversation Beth left the shop, returned to her mother's house to prepare for Alan and Cathy's visit. When that was done she thought she would take herself off for a walk past the weir and the one-time country manor house which had, in more recent years, been used as a home for maladjusted boys. Not two miles away there was a similar home for girls. The thought of the two homes always made her think of the early centuries where monks and nuns lived in close proximity to each other and of the number of clandestine meetings there must have been. No doubt, history was repeating itself with the girls and boys absconding to meet up at every opportunity. The walk would be a good chance to think about all sorts of things.

The walk along the country lanes seemed even more enjoyable as thoughts of the previous evening pervaded Beth's mind. She mentally hugged herself, affording a little smile as she remembered dancing with James to the strains of Strauss. She had felt so safe, so warm, so happy. But there had been something else as well – an old familiar feeling had crept into her consciousness. Now was the time to let it have its moment so that she could think about it and work it out. That feeling was sadness, an incredible sadness; a sadness as deep as the happiness she felt with James.

"The two sides," she thought. "Everything has two sides."

Sadness and happiness, but what was the relevance to her evening with James? Deep down she already knew the answer – the music had been the trigger; she just didn't really want to revisit it. The dream replayed in Beth's mind as clearly as the night she dreamt it. The scene was a large square room, oak panelled, with candle wall sconces all around. The musicians played a waltz and soldiers were dancing in their red and white uniforms, each bearing impressive gold-fringed epaulettes and a sword at the left hip. All the ladies wore beautiful ball gowns. At the top of the steps leading down to the dance floor stood an elegant young woman, dark hair swept up showing her slender neck, wearing a plain but beautiful gown of a striking and shimmering peacock blue. It seemed strange that the hem of the dress was only tacked up, the long temporary stitches clearly visible. The expression on this beautiful woman's face conveyed utter sadness as she gazed at one particular soldier who was dancing with nothing but the spectral haze of a gossamer dress. His face also showed immense sadness, his eyes engaging with nothing. The unspoken message was that this young soldier went into battle after the ball, never to return, leaving unfinished business with the young woman in the blue dress, hence the tacking stitches at the hem. The soldier? He bore an almost exact likeness to Mark and although 'she of the blue dress' bore little resemblance to herself, Beth knew that it was her soul...she could feel the heartbreak of this elegant lady. The situation with Mark had been sorted out by Joe and Tina when they had established that Beth and Mark were true soulmates with the added bonus of a bond tying them together for eternity. So what was the message brought with these reignited feelings? It wasn't the person – Mark – so that only left the situation. Beth pondered the point but only one of several possibilities resonated with her inner knowledge. James had to be someone else for whom she had to do a job; he must have some unfinished business with which only she could help. Whatever it was, she was sure it was her job to lead him somewhere, or to something, and the way things were going she had an inkling that whatever they shared between them at the moment was all part of it. It was likely that she had to guide him to where he was supposed to be and to know him well enough so that when that time came she could leave him there, thus fulfilling some spiritual obligation she was carrying from a previous life. Yet, something didn't quite ring true with that. All she had to do now was to work out what that previous life was if she wanted to fully understand what was going on. And she did want to know – very much.

The interruption to Beth's thoughts was welcome as the emotions of that dream tended to stay with her every time it came to her. Sometimes it surprised her to realise that the feelings were still there but, as she reminded herself, to forget would lay her prone to the full impact of such desolation should it happen again. May God forbid that it ever would. She hoped her theory was correct and that she could distract herself from those thoughts by answering the buzzing of her mobile.

Buzz buzz. Hi B. How are you today? Just wanted to say thank you for your lovely company last night. Hope you slept well – sorry if I stayed too long. It's always a pleasure talking to you. J.

CHAPTER NINE

The next two weeks flew by; the time being occupied with mother, medical appointments and Charlotte returning home, which meant lots of catching up with news and adventures of her time in Canada. Dorothy was as daft as a brush and had provided Charlotte with such interesting and hilarious tales to tell, like how she had been making her way home from the shop one day in January when the snow was very deep. She slipped, couldn't get her footing and ended up crawling on all fours back to the safety of her house. "Good thing I was wearing my snowsuit," she laughed. "The temperature was minus 20."

Charlotte was hooting with laughter as she retold this story to Beth, which then set Beth off, mainly because cousin Dorothy was actually her dad's cousin and was 90 years old.

"My God, she's marvellous – if I get to that age I hope it will be the same for me," chortled Charlotte. "What have you been up to mum? You seem quite a bit more relaxed and happier than when I went on my travels."

"Another month since grandad died love. Time, perhaps, is having a play in it," said Beth. "And I have had lots of support from my friends at the coffee mornings." She paused for a moment before deciding that she should really mention that she saw James at least once a week, and when they didn't they would engage in interesting text conversations. As casually as possible she brought it into the conversation. Charlotte had always been daddy's girl so Beth was a little concerned that she would read into it something that wasn't there.

"Who is he?" she asked, almost icily. "What do Jack and Em say about another man on the scene?"

"It's nothing like that. I think we just clicked as friends, possibly because we are both alone – no spouse, no children at home, no full-time jobs...and we both have music in common. We just enjoy the company," Beth said, purposely forgetting to say that Daniel and Emily didn't know but, then, what was there to know? Nothing. Nevertheless it started Beth thinking and, of all things, thinking about Mark.

What did she feel about this enigmatic man James? Quite a lot, but what exactly? Their sense of humour was much the same and they shared a similar taste in music. They certainly felt very easy together and played word games via text. If he said he was walking past a field full of sheep she would reply that she 'hoped the smell wasn't too ba-aa-ad.'

And he would respond with 'don't lambaste me with funny talk,' to which she would add something like 'but this game is shear genius.' And so it would continue. The last volley had lasted seven hours and saw Beth laughing out loud to herself in some very public places, earning more than one quizzical look. My, she enjoyed those word games. But what was it about James that made her think of Mark? Could he really be another Mark? It didn't feel quite right as the interaction with James was even more intense but on a different level. All the same, if she had to take him somewhere and leave him, where? In Mark's case Beth remembered Sarah asking searching questions about him and making her instrumental in getting them together and that seemed to be the job she had to do for Mark at first – take him somewhere and then step right away from him. Once he and Sarah had paired up it was no longer right for Beth to be in his life so she tried to back off completely. However, the texting and chatting continued, not at her behest. It was so, so difficult to ignore their exclusiveness but to walk away had to be right. She had no place in their life. Then had come the healing session with Joe and Tina and the real purpose of Beth's place in Mark's life had been discovered. This should have happened before meeting Sarah because it was all about making him stand on his own two feet in all respects, including romantic relationships. Obviously, the bond between Mark and Beth was far too strong for either of them to let go, Beth became ill and the drastic measure of the bond being broken had to occur. She went to her desk and pulled out the file on her dreams, specifically the one at the harbour and the man with a crocodile head. She found a pen and paper and googled: 'Egyptian God crocodile head.' It wasn't long before she began writing information down and when she read it all back to herself there was an almost incomprehensible sense of right settling within her. Her notes read:

Sobek, Egyptian God depicted with crocodile head. Old Kingdom of Egypt 2686-2181BC. Name given to 3rd millennium BC when Egypt attained its first continuous peak of civilisation – Lower Nile Valley. Sobek known as God of the Nile, bringing fertility to the land. MARK WAS A FARMER...FERTILITY TO THE LAND!

Parents Khnum and Neith. Khnum, creator God of water, fertility and procreation, patron Deity of Potters...Egyptian mythology says he fashioned human children from straw and clay on a potters wheel and gave them their souls. EXPERIMENTATION OF HUMANISATION AT ATLANTIS!

Temple at Kom Ombo – unusually, a double temple – dedicated to Sobek and Horus. MARK WAS – IS – A GEMINI...TWINS (double)!

Sobek said to have been married to Hathor, Renentutet and two others.

Renentutet was the Snake Goddess depicted with either the head of a cobra or a lion. I WAS BORN IN THE CHINESE YEAR OF THE SNAKE AND AM A LEO!

COULD IT POSSIBLY BE THAT MARK WAS SOBEK AND I WAS RENENTUTET???? Fantasy? Coincidence? Possibility?

Thinking back to the bond, Beth realised that there could have been no other possible course of action than to have it broken. And thank goodness it was, otherwise she would have continued to ignore the abdominal pains, which had been slowly becoming more severe. Within a year the period of grace between the onset of pain and collapse had shortened from 15 minutes to 20 seconds. Where once she would have been able to find somewhere to lie flat and let the pain subside, she then had no time at all. Very inconvenient, as she found out at a checkout one day when she suddenly jackknifed and let out a shout of pain. It frightened the cashier and Beth realised that she needed to do something about it. An ovarian cyst was eventually discovered but because it was on the same side as one she'd had exactly 30 years earlier, and there was the risk of something sinister going on, it was decided to carry out a full hysterectomy. That now meant Beth had been subjected to three abdominal surgical procedures: ovarian cyst as a teenager; C-Section with Charlotte; and then the hysterectomy. The first two had been lateral incisions, so only one scar, but the third had been a vertical incision, which was not pretty. Actually, it made her think of the poor souls who, in times long ago, had been subjected to being hanged, drawn and quartered.

That, in turn, brought another past life dream to mind. The young monk who was hanged for nothing. Again, it had been like watching a short video. He looked so young, about 19, and sat so serenely, head bowed, eyes closed. His face looked so pale against his rich brown hair and his dark, coarse, woollen habit. Had his eyes been open he would have seen the gallows, the earthen open area and the first strains of sunlight beginning to light the day. So, it was early morning, very early morning. The scene was completely void of people, which was uncommon for what appeared to be a very public hanging. Void except for a jester dressed in a green, long-sleeved, close-fitting top with a short 'folded' swirly yellow skirt, complete with the typical tight leggings and pointed hat with bells. He was laughing and cartwheeling in front of the gallows. Knowledge told her that this was, indeed, no ordinary hanging; the gallows were so close to the stone wall of the room the young man was in that they could have been attached. No buildings or street vendors were visible, just a high wall with an open gateway surrounding the outside earthen area. This could easily have been an enclosed building such as...what? A castle? A tower? Then the voice saying, "It's a shame, the hanging is in a minute," entered the dream and Beth remembered every single thing about that dream, just like the others, even knowing without being told that it was somewhere in the time frame of 900-1100AD. So, what was this one all about? Her immediate translation was that the man, an older monk, behind the voice was regretful of the hanging but did not, or could not, do anything to stop it. The jester was either employed to sneer at the young monk or, worse, was the force behind the hanging. Or perhaps it was symbolic of some trickery behind it all. Why were there no spectators? Was it an illegal hanging? Oh, this one was not nice and Beth was not unhappy to think that she may never fully understand the whys and wherefores of it.

"Mum, I'm going over to Juliet's, OK? Probably won't be back until late," said Charlotte as she stuck her head round the door.

"OK, love," answered Beth. "Give my love to Juliet. Have a good time."

As usual, she felt a little wrung out after thinking about the young monk so she picked up her mobile and started tapping.

Write message: How are you doing? Hug. B. Press send.

Buzz buzz. Would you like to join me for tea? I'll pick you up if you like. Hig 4u2. J.

Buzz buzz. Hug 4u2. J

Write message: That would be very nice – thank you. It's OK, I'll make my own way – can't have you running all over the place like that. What time? B. Press send.

Buzz buzz. Whenever you like. We could play some piano if you like. Will you have time to stay a while? I do enjoy your company. Hug. J

Write message: OK. Will text you when leaving here, but will probably be about 5pm. Won't take long to reach you. Piano would be good. I enjoy your company too. Thanks, c u later. B. Press send.

Beth found herself really looking forward to going to James's for the evening. She had time to get ready too, which was a bonus. There was nothing urgent she had to do...she'd been to the bank, done the ironing, made a cake and some of those gorgeous ginger cookies and peanut butter cookies. Cookies were easy to make and Beth enjoyed doing them, which was just as well as Charlotte and Daniel always devoured them with such speed that a large batch barely lasted two days! As she wasn't seeing Daniel for a few days it seemed that things had worked out just right and she could take some over to James. The sound of her front door opening was not an unwelcome noise to her otherwise calm mind. It was only 2pm and plenty of time for getting ready.

"Hello? Beth? It's Michael."

"Hello Michael, is everything OK, only you never come over on a Monday?" questioned Beth as she automatically put the kettle on to make a cup of tea.

Michael made plenty of small talk about Charlotte and Daniel but when the inevitable lull in the conversation came his shoulders slumped and his eyes fell to the table then back up to hold Beth's questioning gaze. "I can't fool you, can I Beth?" he asked. "You know me too well, even after all our years apart."

Panic rose in her chest as she thought with horror that he was going to ask to come back to her and, after all, he was still her husband. Oh, why hadn't she asked for a divorce long ago?

Michael took a deep breath, held it for a moment and then let it go. "I have something to tell you and I want to tell you before I tell the children. Cancer, Beth, I have cancer, and it isn't looking good – maybe a year. I just wanted to say how sorry I am for the way things turned out between us. I know it was all my fault. I was a bad husband and absent father, and then Pauline – I couldn't have done things worse, really."

With the panic still within she said, "You weren't a bad husband...just absent, and we drifted apart too far to recover."

"Beth, you are too nice for your own good," Michael answered genuinely. "And most of all I want to say, well, thank you doesn't cover it, but thank you for never turning your back on me. As daft as this may sound, I am truly grateful for you never having asked for a divorce. I can't explain why but that is giving me help to see this thing through. Thank you Beth. You deserve so much more than I ever gave you, and I deserve so much less."

Beth didn't have to add anything to the conversation; this needed to be a one-way chat. Michael had a lot to say and he wanted to do it all in one go, this much she recognised. He explained how everything between him and Pauline was fine and how they had discussed his care plan. Pauline was going to do as much of the care as she could but at the end, Michael told her, he would go into a hospice, as he didn't want to put that level of stress on her, or anyone else for that matter. In a hospital environment there would be a team of people to share the load. They talked, and cried, for well over an hour, coming out of the encounter with laughter and an understanding that sat happily with the both of them. Michael left her feeling happier than he had done so for ages and Beth felt a certain peace.

4:40pm and she was as ready as she would ever be, hair tied back in a loose plait, jeans, smart shirt and very practical flat shoes. Nothing special but it all worked together and she didn't look a mess. What's more, she had make-up on for a change. All she had to do was grab a jacket and go. No, not a jacket – too stuffy. Jumper. The light bluebell blue fluffy one would be OK – not her newest jumper but it was very comfy and the colour suited her well. It was more like an old friend than a jumper.

Write message: On my way. B Press send.

James answered the door, smiled widely and invited Beth into his home. "You look nice," he said. "I've just boiled the kettle – would you like a cup of tea? I'm having one."

"In that case, yes please...um...I've brought you some cookies...I hope you like them."

To her total surprise James turned, wrapped his arms around her and planted a kiss on her cheek and then held her in a tight hug. "Thank you, Beth...you lovely girl..." and then there was the second kiss on the cheek. Beth found her arms around him too and it felt, in truth, ...warm...good...lovely. They seemed to stand there interlocked for a long time, each taking something from the other. Was it her thoughts of 'What do I do with this?' and 'Oh, Lord' that broke the spell?

"Um...tea?" James asked as he gently let go and turned towards the kettle. Everything then carried on as though that moment hadn't happened; yet both knew it had. They had a very enjoyable evening eating and chatting about everything and James found himself opening up to Beth, talking more and more about Holly, Laura and his new job at the college. Beth found it easy to listen to him. Then the fun began.

"How about a bit of piano?" James asked. "Let's see what you can do," he said laughing.

Beth knew she was woefully short of his standards and warned him accordingly but he was having none of it. "My hands are a bit cold," she said. "Let me put my jumper on and get warmed up first."

To James the act of pulling the jumper over her head and threading her arms into the sleeves seemed to play out in slow motion and as Beth's head popped through the neckline she saw the softest look in his eyes. But she chose to ignore it.

"That's nice," he said, so quietly it would have been missed by anyone standing more than a step away. And then a little louder, "I like your fluffy jumper." The soft look had been replaced by one which said, 'I hope you didn't see that.' But it was too late for James; his hands had already gone out and were smoothing her arms.

Reading his eyes, Beth calmly brought in the mood of level-headedness by saying, "Right, ready. What am I, or we, to play? Are you going to play something for me to hear, please?" She was left to look through his music books to find a piece she felt happy to play and he sat at his piano and just let his hands bring the instrument to life. No written music, he was making it up as he went along, and it was beautiful. She watched his hands on the keys, and then studied his face. He was lost in his music. This was so beautiful to witness, and she could have stood there, watching, for a million years. The music stirred within her and she also became lost in it. When he stopped it was almost 10 minutes later. He looked at Beth's face – those eyes – what was it he could see in there? She had gone somewhere...where? What was that look? Was it sorrow? Quietly he slipped out into the kitchen and five minutes later brought back two cups of tea. By now she was sitting with her eyes closed. James put his hand on her shoulder so very gently, barely making contact, and Beth's head automatically moved to rest on his arm. He said nothing and a few seconds later her eyes opened and he looked again. It was, indeed, a great sadness he could see, and in an instant it was gone, replaced by a look of apology. The tea was the perfect solution.

"Where did you go Beth?" he asked.

"I have no idea," she answered convincingly. Actually, she did know where she had gone and she knew what she'd felt. Definitely not for James's ears. Oh, no, no, no. She couldn't possibly tell him that.

With tea break over, they decided to have a go at playing a duet or two. Beth hadn't played duets since her days with her piano teacher decades ago and she remembered with fondness Mrs. Nex, a lady so laid back there was nowhere to fall. She always looked as though she had come in from the garden, that lovely lady whose smile always said, 'nothing to worry about'.

"This would be interesting. Let's try this one," suggested James. Rossini's Barber of Seville.

"Oh, wonderful," grinned Beth. "I've never played it in my life and, on looking at it, please may I play the bass part?"

"You can – just don't go too fast! And you get to do the pedal, of course," replied James.

A horrified look crossed Beth's face. "No! No pedal! I hate the pedal! Please don't make me do the pedal," she begged. "Especially when there will be mistakes everywhere."

"Ah! So I have a challenge on my hands, do I?" he said laughing. "OK, today I'll do the pedal, but I'll get you doing pedal yet. You ready, you little minx?"

And off they went, Beth completely unco-ordinated, James being very, very patient, the pair of them laughing uncontrollably. And so the evening went until, inevitably, Beth had to go home.

"Come and do this again?" James asked.

"If you'd like me to," said Beth.

"Yes, please. We had a lot of fun didn't we? I do love your company Beth."

She felt so sad to be leaving him that night. He gave her an enormous hug and then...then...ohhh...the soft kiss on the neck. Everything in her body trembled at the tenderness of this one kiss. Then there was another one. A murmur that Beth truly hoped was inaudible escaped from her throat and her arms found themselves around James's neck.

"I'm lost, completely lost," she whispered to herself. And then it happened. His gorgeous mouth found hers and they shared the most wonderful, passionate kiss. There was softness, urgency, the gentle explorations of a first kiss mingled with the appreciation of a kiss so well known to each, all mixed together at the same time. They drew apart, Beth looking almost scared.

"I'm sorry," James said. "It was only a moment."

"Pity," Beth whispered, without even thinking about what she was saying. Had she looked into James's eyes she might have understood why she said it. Without a second thought, he took her into his arms again, and she went very willingly, this time their lips meeting with an urgency that only two lovers who had been parted from each other for a very long time would share. Their hands caressed each other as though they were so familiar with the body they touched, Beth not really needing James to guide her hand to his pulsating excitement, and not hesitating to respond when he, so gently, took her breast in his hand and drew his thumb over her nipple.

"We can't," choked Beth. "We mustn't. This can't happen."

They shared a long embrace, both wishing it to never end, clinging to each other with hope and longing. When, eventually, they let go and with sadness evident in both faces, they shared a chaste goodnight kiss and Beth left. She got in her car to drive home through water that no windscreen wiper could help with. She cried and cried and cried.

James sat at the piano again and played, as when Beth was there, just letting the music come into his head and out through his fingers. It was so sad.

Early the following morning her mobile came to life.

Buzz buzz. Hi, Beth. I'm sorry if I crossed any boundaries. Are you OK? Sorry if I've woken you too early...couldn't sleep...needed to say this. J

Beth sighed with relief. She thought that maybe she had scared James and she would never hear from him again or, if she did, it would be awkward to say the least.

Write message: Hi Maestro. I'm fine, thanks. What about you? Thank you for a lovely evening – no boundaries crossed, not by you anyway. We'll be OK. I haven't slept too well either. Press send.

Buzz buzz. It was a really lovely evening, I had the best time. Please say you will come over again some time soon." J.

Write message: Of course I will come over again. Or you could come over to me. Press send.

Buzz buzz. This evening? J

Excitement seemed to race around her body and Beth replied,

"Tonight is good. You come to me."

And neither knew, but both felt the same way. "I wish...."

CHAPTER TEN

Hazel was replenishing the shelves in the shop when Beth walked in and picked up a basket for the items she needed for both herself and her mother. As she slowly made her way around the aisles a feeling of being watched washed over her, unpleasantly so but, determined not to be intimidated, she carried on without showing any hint of disquiet. She made her way to the till hoping to be served by Georgina but Hazel quickly appeared saying, "I'll serve Mrs. Channing, Georgina...perhaps you would like to take your break now?" and she gave Beth a long, unblinking stare with eyes almost as dark as tar. The verbal stress on the 'Mrs.' had not been lost on Beth and this was the second nudge to her consciousness to stay neutral and unfazed by anything that might follow, as surely something would...it had that feel to it.

"Did you find everything you needed?" came the statutory comment to all shoppers, followed by, "Having a guest or two?"

"Yes, thank you, I have everything I came in for," answered Beth, deliberately not answering the second question. She thought she knew where this was leading.

"Isn't James a lovely man? We had a very nice evening together on Thursday – we get on so well; we're very close. How is your husband?" Hazel asked, putting another stress on the word 'husband' and without even trying to disguise her smugness and derision for Beth.

"Michael is the same as ever thanks," answered Beth with a huge smile on her face. "Oh, and may I have a couple of scratch cards – a number 9 and a number 11 – thank you." She got her debit card ready for inserting into the machine. "Must get back to mother – she'll be waiting for her morning coffee," said Beth, making it clear that she was not going to indulge Hazel in inane conversation. "Thank you very much," she said in her usual happy and casual way before heading off into the street and back to mother. She couldn't look back but she knew that the angular, chisel-faced Hazel was still boring her eyes into Beth's back. "Aha!" she thought to herself. "So we have a big dose of the green eye, do we? OK. Got the measure of you Hazel."

It had been a simple day with mother so Beth decided to drive into town for a bit of window shopping at the very least. As she strolled towards Debenhams she caught sight of Alison struggling along with shopping, which didn't seem to want to accompany her. Alison stopped, abandoned her efforts and flopped on to the bench beside her and covered her face with her hands.

"Alison?" ventured Beth as she unwittingly rubbed her abdomen. "Whatever is wrong? Can I help?"

"Oh, hello lass. That bloody man! I tell you – I'm going back to work," came the reply in a watered down Yorkshire accent.

Beth decided to keep quiet to see if the rest of the story came out of its own accord. It did.

"All he does is chase me around the house… 'Do you know that if you wash clothes at 30 instead of 40 it will make a saving of XXXX pounds a year? If you wait until the ironing bin is absolutely full you won't have to switch the iron on and off so many times in a month. Don't boil the kettle until you are ready to make the tea. We could save a bit if you would…' and then he follows me like a sticky shadow and switches off the lights when I walk out of a room, even though we have energy saving bulbs – what a waste of space they are – and no matter if I am going back in that room within a minute. I tell you, if poor old Mr. Bradley across the way watched our lights going on and off as they do he'd be having seizures left, right and centre. And THEN he decided he was going to do the cooking, but will he put a lid on saucepans? The bloody 'eck he will! Bloody accountant, bloody penny pinching with everything yet, apparently,

APPARENTLY, according to the laws of St. Bloody Bernie, putting a lid on a saucepan would not be of benefit. Ee, I'm sorry lass..." and Alison burst out into fits of giggles. "Ee, that did me good."

Beth flashed the broadest grin, announced she desperately needed a wee and was heading for Debenhams; would Alison like to join her? Off they both went to do what only women do best – go for a wee and then visit the cafeteria for a cup of tea and a piece of cake.

Alison and Beth relaxed in their guilty pleasure of staring at two enormous pieces of creamy confection knowing that, before long, they would both be feeling very full indeed. It was almost like Christmas Eve where the excitement of anticipation was better than anything, yet was so agonising. Why was that, Beth wondered? She thought of the wonderful scene in the film *Love Actually* between Daniel and his stepson, Sam, where Sam says, 'Something worse? What can be worse than the total agony of being in love?' This brought Daniel to agreeing that being in love was, indeed, total agony. Much the same principle, concluded Beth. Being in love brought with it all the anticipation of lovely things to come but also the agony of knowing that it could be gone at any time through death, another person or, as in her case, just drifting apart. That's what eating cake was like...the anticipation of the lovely taste coupled with the agony of knowing that all too soon it would be consumed and gone.

"You look lost in thought, lass," said Alison. "What is occupying your mind? It wouldn't be James, now, would it? Only, I know you two are quite close."

That made Beth laugh out loud and she told Alison exactly what had been occupying her mind.

"Ee, you do think some strange things," said Alison. "But, I have to agree with you there."

"Shall we have another when this lot's gone? Just to lift the agony, of course!" Beth added in quickly to deflect the question about James, because she really didn't know what to think on that score. There certainly was a muddle going on in that mind of hers somewhere but exactly why was as clear as mud. She seemed to be at some kind of crossroads; the house would soon be emptier than usual with Charlotte away at uni, mother was beginning to pull her down with all the negativity she discharged Beth's way and there was nothing she could do to stop it. Michael was making some really unnerving noises but, this much she did know, those noises were definitely not what she wanted to hear. Then there was James. Yes, they both had enormous fun and she really enjoyed their times together. In fact, she realised that every day she looked forward to the next time they could laugh together. They were good for each other in that way. She might text him later and see if he would like to have coffee somewhere one day soon. If James was missing from her life what would she actually have left? Everything she had before, obviously, but what exactly was that?

"Alison?" ventured Beth. "Can I ask you something?"

"Aye, lass, of course you can – anything. It sounds a bit serious though...thee got a problem?"

Beth took a breath and continued. "Have you spoken to Frankie lately? Only, I've been telling her some stuff recently and she thinks I should share it with some of you. I'm wondering if she finds it too strange, or even onerous, to be the only one to hear it. I have read about it in the past and Emily has even confirmed it with first hand accounts...times when nurses have seen death...actually passed it in the corridor or met it coming out of a ward."

Alison was nodding gently and she explained that she'd actually had the very same experience at one of the care homes she had worked at in Yorkshire – and had even met ghosts. She didn't know how else to put it; to say she had been in a time warp sounded a little far-fetched, she thought.

Beth asked that she would very much like to know about anything she could tell her.

Alison continued: "Well, I were walking along by the River Wharfe in Tadcaster with my dear old dog, Lucy, and I saw a bunch of about 10 teenagers walking towards me but they weren't dressed quite right for now, their clothes were more 1940s or 50s. They were looking at Lucy, not me, and as I went towards them they started to walk backwards – not turning around – literally walking backwards – they were still looking at my dog – they couldn't see me at all. Anyway, I ended up walking right through them, not in between them – it felt a bit tingly. Ee, I've had a few experiences like that. There was another time I were at M&S and I saw a man who was dressed in what I assumed were Victorian clothes. His hat was like a tall bowler hat and he had one of them scarf things round his neck, a workingman's shirt wi' black trousers and jacket. He were slim and about 5 feet 6 inches. Nobody else was looking at him yet he stuck out like a sore thumb. I mentioned it to Malcolm and he told me that M&S was built on the old brewery site so he thought the man was probably a brewery worker from those times. Want another one?" she asked Beth as she lifted the teapot.

"Yes, please...it is good to hear of someone else who has these experiences," answered Beth and Alison continued with another experience.

"I'd gone for an interview at a care home in York. It turned out that all the staff had walked out because the company wouldn't pay more for the hard work they did. Anyway, I needed whatever money I could earn then so I carried on wi' interview and I were taken up a beautiful staircase and shown the rooms. In one of them I were introduced to Lady somebody-or-other, but it were such a large room and a bit dark so I couldn't see anyone. As I went home I considered if I would be able to cope wi' driving there in the winter when it were foggy or icy but decided, yes I would, mainly because I needed the income. Well, that night I had a dream where I were walking around the house and had reached the Lady's bedroom when from the left came a girl of about 12 years old – ringlets and dressed well. I were about to go into the room and she said, 'You can't go in there' and she turned into what I can only describe as a thing from hell. I can tell you I wasted no time in ringing the nursing home the next day to decline the job, saying the roads would be too dangerous in winter. They understood because they were familiar with the area. A couple of days later I went for another interview. The matron who interviewed me, believe it or not, was one of the staff who had walked out of the home I've just told you about. Ee, she were a nice lady and I told her about my dream and to my horror she simply said, 'Odd...it normally stays in the kitchen'. So what do you reckon Frankie could be struggling with? I haven't seen her to hear anything."

Beth pulled her senses together after hearing that and thanked Alison for telling her and looked forward to hearing more stories. She didn't want to go into everything too quickly so she merely said that she'd had some dreams, two types of dreams, some of which were of past lives and some which were...um...not. She explained, "I've been gradually telling Frankie about the past life dreams and that seemed to be OK, but she asked if I had told any of you guys and it is beginning to weigh a bit on my mind. I think the time has come for me to share the other dreams but feel I have to be careful who I share them with."

"You'll be all right wi' me, lass. I've had kids, you can't scare me!" said Alison. "I'm all ears if you would like to tell me. Now then, lass, get it off your chest."

Beth gave the biggest sigh and began. "Do you remember...no, of course you wouldn't...you weren't around these parts then. This happened locally...a child went missing and was never found – and has still not been found either alive or...not. I had a dream, a still-picture dream, and in this dream was a place, a man, a child and an axe."

Alison remained silent, listening intently.

"The child's wrists were together as though bound with rope – that was the thought – rope; not tape, rope – but there was no rope visible. The hands were not there either, apparently chopped off, which is possibly why the axe was in the picture. The child's face was contorted with the unbearable pain of torture. The man was her father. The place was a dusty log cabin, one room from what I could see, with a large table/bench in it. He was behind it with the heels of his hands on the edge of the table, fingers curled underneath, arms straight, staring directly with piercing, defiant eyes, at me as the observer."

Alison took up the silence. "I suppose it was such a distressing thing to happen in a rural community like this that the story would play on everyone's mind. But you are trying to tell me something else, I think. Do you feel like carrying on?"

"In for a penny, in for a pound," said Beth. "The child disappeared three weeks after I dreamt it. The pictures in the newspapers were exactly as I had seen in the dream; the child was wearing the same clothes as reported and the hair and age was the same. The father, although older and with longer hair, was identical even down to the glasses he was wearing. It affected me so much that I became scared. I mean, what could I have done with it? It made me feel that maybe I'd missed something and that I could have prevented it, yet there were no specifics. I didn't recognise the child or the father. Neither did I recognise the cabin. All I could get from it was that a child had either been murdered or separated from the family or father in some way. The missing hands; why would the arms have been bound up? Why the dreadful contortion of the face if it hadn't been murder? And the look on the father's face, lord, that was so scary. The newspaper pictures of them both showed them clearly as the same two in my dream," finished Beth. "What could I have done Alison? Do you think there was anything I could have done? I hadn't discovered the Spiritualist Church then so didn't know Malcolm; this was several decades ago by the way."

Alison wasn't in the least bit aghast at what Beth had just told her and quietly said, "There was nothing you could have done with that information lass, but the question I suspect you have asked yourself is why did you have the dream at all? What was the point of showing it to you? It was certainly awful for you to experience. I'm not sure I can provide any answers right now but I will certainly think on it."

"It wasn't a pleasant realisation to see something like that," continued Beth. "But what makes it a whole load worse is that I have had five similar dreams, each one of them reported nationally exactly three weeks afterwards. The information became a little more definite I suppose, yet still not enough to do anything with and, yes, I have wondered endlessly why the dreams happened. There were three within a year and the other two at random times. One was in the 80s, a sectarian killing in Ireland. A young man was being frogmarched across a desolate piece of grassland, grasped by men on either side of him. He was forced to kneel and he was shot." Beth touched the lower left part of the back of her head. "I actually felt the bullet go in, Alison. It was like a dull pain

– obviously nothing like he would have felt but nevertheless I definitely felt it. Scary."

"I think you really need to open this up to the group, Beth. This is fascinating stuff and I am sure Malcolm will have some guidance for you. Maybe you need to join another development circle – a rescue circle or something. My understanding is not nearly as far forward as Malcolm's but I am ready to hear as much as you want to tell me. You said the information became a little more definite or clear wi' some of the dreams. How?" questioned Alison, hoping that Beth would continue. The ever-practical Yorkshire woman pointed out that there was enough tea left in their teapots for another so they might just as well have their money's worth. With tea poured and plates empty, Beth continued with her next dream.

"This was also like a photograph and I suppose it is not quite right to say there was information with it, but I seemed to glean information via the symbolism. The dream showed an empty room with sunlight flooding through a window onto plain floorboards – not polished ones – and there was an old tin bath filled with water and a body with a knife in its back floating within. It was a small tin bath so the body had to be small, yet it was a man, not a child. I don't know how I knew that, but that was the information that came through with it. Well, actually, yes, I did understand how I could have knowledge without hearing or seeing...oh, I'm not making any sense! In my past life dreams the same thing happened – the knowledge was planted in my head but not by words. Anyway, so I had an empty room, sunlight, small adult stabbed and floating in his bath. Again, exactly three weeks later, the news came through of a man being found, stabbed, in his bath. He was discovered by a carer who had arrived to carry out duties. The man lived alone, was profoundly deaf and was small in stature. I took the bare floorboards to indicate living alone and the deafness to be indicated by the sunlight and the emptiness of the room. It is said that if you lose one sense another is heightened, so maybe because he couldn't hear he had very clear eyesight. Or perhaps the sunlight just represented the fact he was found the next morning."

Beth picked up her cup as Alison said, "Yes, I can follow the symbolism when you say it like that. Gosh, how your mind works! You said that was your second dream...what about the third one? Du'st want to go on with that one?"

Beth put down her cup, folded her arms over the table and said, "Well, I might as well tell you now I've come this far...and then we'll get some retail therapy. This is the one which probably had the most information in it, but again not direct information. This was a moving picture dream, like watching a film. The place was a hospital with a long corridor with single rooms on one side, each occupied by a man. There were rooms on the opposite side but they were more like toilets, bathrooms, or offices – not rooms as in bedrooms or side wards. It was a strange layout for a hospital as there were no large wards, just single rooms, but a hospital it was. Three nurses dressed in completely white uniforms, dresses with buttons down the front, complete with old fashioned white headpieces that hung at the back in a typical kite shape. They looked rather like nuns in short white uniforms and were marching up the corridor. Someone shouted, 'He's done it again,' and at the end of the corridor there was a shower room and I was shown a young girl of about 18 with shoulder length brown hair taking a shower but there was a knife in her back. I could only see her top half."

Alison said nothing as Beth looked at her with that haunted look in her eyes.

Beth continued: "As before, exactly three weeks later the story broke of a 17-year-old girl, with shoulder length brown hair, found semi naked, stabbed in the back, in the doorway of a Catholic Church which stood in the grounds of a psychiatric hospital. It had been raining."

Alison picked the conversation up. "So the girl was exactly as shown – dark hair, age, and I guess seeing her in the shower to the waist was the indicator of her being found semi-naked...and of the rain. The nurses, who looked like nuns, actually represented the Catholic Church and the single rooms pointed to it being a psychiatric hospital rather than a general hospital."

"That's about it," agreed Beth.

"Well, lass," Alison concluded. "You really should tell Malcolm, you know. There must be some reason why you were given these dreams. I can see it still bothers you from time to time. My guess is you try to tuck it away somewhere in that mind of yours and you are pretty successful at it on the whole, but every now and again out it pops and starts you thinking all over again – am I right? He's quite good, you know, our Malcolm."

Beth, without realising it, pressed her abdomen, earning the comment from Alison: "Ee, that were filling wa'n't it lass."

With all the tea gone and Beth having agreed to speak to Malcolm, the two of them got up and headed for the loos again before hitting the High Street. This time, Alison's shopping was quite happy to accompany her and gave her no trouble at all. Not only that, St. Bloody Bernie had been kicked into touch. He wasn't going to bother Alison again this week, not now she had all of this to think about. Yes, she might even go home and switch on all the lights in the house just to annoy him. And she might put on a load of washing tomorrow at 40 degrees or, better still, put on a boil wash. The thought of that made her happy, very happy, indeed.

Beth was happy because tomorrow she would be seeing James again and she felt she had a new understanding of what was happening. She had done it before, she could do it again. If James was another Mark then she would let him go, just as she did with Mark. The thing to decide now was whether to tell James what she thought was going on or not. If she didn't tell him he might not understand many things that would happen, and if she did tell him he might still not understand...yes, of course he would, his family had been spiritualists for a number of years...of course he would understand what she was saying. Then she began to worry about how to bring the subject up without referring back to the...the...the...the... 'moment'...they shared. They were just two people who needed that moment at that time, that was all. He was obviously missing Laura and his daughter, Holly, even though he saw her every weekend either at his home or at his in-laws' place. Ray and June sounded such lovely people who cared very deeply for their granddaughter and their son-in-law equally; maybe the care they could give to Holly and James helped them more than anyone could guess. To lose a child, no matter what their age, must be one of the more difficult things in life to encounter. Actually, it was a perfect solution to all their griefs even though it looked as if James was the one who lost most, his wife having died and his daughter living with her grandparents. James was doing his best to now make a good standard of life for Holly by finding a better job and a highly rated school where Holly would receive the education to show her how to hone her intelligence in the best possible way. Ray and June were helping them both by providing a loving and secure home for Holly until James was sorted out. James and Holly were, in return, helping Ray and June by being there whilst they grieved for their daughter. They would be a close and loving family always and Beth wondered how many families were blessed in that way. It would be so easy to shut down after such a tragedy and shut everyone else out, but not for these guys, they were in it together forever.

CHAPTER ELEVEN

The ironing seemed to be taking forever to do – she could tell Charlotte was home again but it didn't matter one little bit...Beth was happy to do mumsie things for her daughter for the short time left before uni beckoned. The time had flown by and it was only a few days before she would be leaving her beautiful daughter in the halls of residence at the University of Southampton and she wondered how much she would see of her after that dreaded day. It was on a par with leaving her children at pre-school for the first time actually. She recalled the mums who walked away from the pre-school doors to go home alone with tears flooding down their faces; some were quite justified as their little ones screamed or cried as their mums left them with all those other children. Daniel had looked at her with sad eyes but had not cried; her brave little warrior she called him. She had expected Charlotte to give her a quick backward glance and a wave of her tiny hand but, in fact, she had surprised her mum by giving her a lip wobble instead. She thought of another child who had been brave, like Daniel, when faced with a challenge, a long, long, long time ago. Centuries ago.

The tunnel was of deep orange sandy soil and it led to a gladiatorial arena where the sun was blindingly strong. Hmm, middle of the day and it was very cool in the tunnel, yet out in the arena it was very hot; the word Ancona silently boomed out...all this unspoken knowledge. There was a recess in the tunnel wall and in it stood a king and his queen, both dressed in white floor length togas, his edged with gold around the neck and down the front. She had gold ornamentation in her hair, earrings and a large brooch at the left shoulder. The togas fell in regimented folds so the fabric must have been fairly heavy. In front of them stood a boy, no more than 10 or 12-years-old. He was dressed in a short toga with pleated skirt, clearly of good quality, and he carried a shield and a broad sword. He faced the king and queen, the king looking at him with reserved pride, but the queen looking slightly away with an air of aloofness or even haughtiness. More unspoken knowledge said that this was father and son and the message was clear. The boy was to go into the arena, but he wouldn't come out alive. How could any parent send their child to their death?

This dream had bothered Beth for years; she eventually googled Ancona and, finding there was an Ancona in Italy, her search widened into the geography of the place and its kings. Surely, Italy would have been ruled by an emperor rather than a king? The geographical search confirmed the red sandy soil and, more surprisingly, confirmed that Italy did indeed have kings, the first of which appeared to be the Heruli leader, Odoacer. Recalling the dream, Beth realised she had never recognised anything or any of the people in it, except that the boy had dark curly hair like Daniel's had turned out as he became a young man. As she was thinking about it the image of the soldier at the ball floated past her vision, the soldier who had been the very image of Mark. "Oh! My good God!" thought Beth. The hair, shape of face, the colouring – was it as she thought, could it possibly be?

The ironing done and the clothes put away, Beth did what she always did when she needed to think and that was to make a cup of tea and have a chocolate biscuit. "What to do with this one?" she asked the kitchen walls knowing she wouldn't get an answer but, then again, truth can be stranger than fiction and in the quest for truth some very strange things can happen. The telephone ringing wasn't particularly odd but the conversation she had with the caller was.

"Hello? Mrs. Channing?" came an unfamiliar voice. "My name is Valerie Summers and I would like to talk to you about your dreams, if you are agreeable."

So taken by surprise was Beth that she found it difficult to formulate sensible or coherent questions and could only ask, "How do you know about them? Who are you?"

"I believe you have a friend, Alison, whose son lives here in Canada..."

"Are you calling from Canada?" queried Beth, feeling a little idiotic for asking the obvious.

"Yes, Alison's son lives in Canada...in fact, both her sons live in Canada." Valerie picked up the conversation. "My son, Darren, works with Paul and they have been alive with tales of your dreams. I am a clairvoyant and over the past week I have been told by our friends in the other world to contact you. Not long ago the message came particularly strong so, here I am my dear, talking to you and not really knowing why it has to be. That information has to come from you. I hope I have not worried or scared you in any way...I understand that you are part of the Spiritualist Church and I know that you have more understanding than perhaps you think."

Beth relaxed a little and the more they chatted and got to know about each other the conversation edged into that of friends catching up with news. She then suggested to Valerie that perhaps she would like to have a FaceTime call so that they could see each other, a suggestion that was readily taken up. Valerie made that call because it was she who needed to talk to Beth for some reason. It had been a good decision as to see each other cemented the beginnings of a good friendship, so when the question of why Valerie had been urged so strongly to ring her that day arose it took no more than a minute for Beth to say that as she had been doing the ironing her thoughts had wandered again to a dream that had never really made any sense until a realisation – or was it just a thought? – had hit home with the precision of a perfectly aimed arrow.

She related the dream set in Ancona of the king, queen and the boy to Valerie and whilst doing so drew the scene with remarkable accuracy of distance, clothes, faces, etc., and held it up for her to see. Valerie closed her eyes briefly then began speaking.

"This is the reason I have to speak with you," she said and carried on without any interruption from Beth. "These people in this dream are all relevant to you now and you have to understand why. Let me link in properly and let's see where it takes us. The king...this man was quite prominent in your life, and the queen...she was not happy with it. I see you as a servant dressed in a bluebell coloured dress of the times...you were servant to the queen. Oh dear...oh, this is not...I see the king taking you as, of course, would have been his right back then to take his wife's servant, and you becoming pregnant. OK, that's what it is...she didn't have children with the king...but you did. Oh, honey, you know these people..." and Valerie's intuitive link came to an end.

Beth was silent for a moment then quietly said, "Yes. Yes, I believe I do know these people. One for sure, because of a physical likeness and I can't have put that likeness into the dream because I had the dream at least 20 years before meeting the person – any of them."

Valerie jumped in with "Well, you were obviously shown that particular face so that you would recognise him when you met him. It WAS the king, wasn't it? He is the one you now recognise?"

Beth was taken aback at Valerie's knowledge and stammered a confirmation. "How…how...how do you know that?"

This made the Canadian woman smile, a knowing smile, and with a chuckling voice she said, "The link between you both is so strong, honey. There is a very real reason why you two have had to meet, so is there anything you want to ask or tell me? Remember, he is not the only one you may have to recognise, but he is the one you are required to recognise. This is Spirit talking to you and there is nothing you can do but take notice. This has happened for a reason, you know. I believe you have something to sort out with this person."

Beth's fingers went to her mouth and danced there for a few seconds before she cleared her throat, crossed her arms and rested them on the table. After swallowing hard she told Valerie that the king was, indeed, someone who had recently come into her life and that she was, she thought, becoming increasingly fond of this man although there wasn't and wouldn't be anything other than friendship between them; she briefly explained their separate situations.

"Don't be too sure about that, my dear. Strange things happen when you aren't looking. If it is meant to be, then it will be; there will be nothing you can do to stop it and if you try then it will keep bringing you back to it, or it back to you. Don't make life any harder than it need be...you will know if and when it is right to give in to the situation. I feel this man is here to make good what he got wrong before, so watch and learn. Whatever you do, do not tell him what you know. Don't forget, he probably has no idea of any of this, so just let it play itself out and go with the flow. Spirit is telling me you must remember that you'll most likely know more characters than just him, so don't be too trusting. If you do as I say – watch and learn – you will be all right.

Valerie paused a short while and studied Beth's face. "Something is bothering you, honey, what is it? I promised you could ask me anything."

This was all the encouragement Beth needed to tell her about the dream of the monk who was hanged, all the while – and out of camera shot – pressing into her abdomen and leaning slightly forward because of a pain which was just going to have to go. "I really can't make any sense of this one at all, Valerie, except I have an overriding feeling that my soul and that of the monk are one and the same and that seems, to me, to be reinforced by the fact that I have always suffered dreadfully with tonsillitis or sore throats and the back of my neck often aches for no apparent reason."

It was Valerie's turn to think now and she began to look at both that dream and that of the king and queen. It didn't take long for her to find common factors between the two without being guided by Spirit. "In the dream of Ancona we had the manipulative queen, the king who wouldn't speak out and the servant who was the target – the queen was beyond jealous of her. In the monk dream it looks as though there are only two key players but, in actual fact, there are three because the voice is the third. What is it he says? 'It's a shame, the hanging is in a minute?' That to me says this was someone who had the chance to say something to stop it but didn't. The empty 'town square' tells me that this was not a public hanging but something done in private, and the cartwheeling jester tells me that this was someone who was highly delighted that the young monk was paying a penalty not warranted. This jester was probably the cause of the hanging, and either had some kind of grudge against the monk or would have benefited by seeing him dead. In both dreams you have the same three players; the one who caused, the one who stood back and watched, and the victim. In both, you have been the victim or target of the malice...oh, OK, OK...I hear you...here is the confirmation from the other side...not only do you play the same part in each dream, so do the other two. Oh, honey, if you recognise the other one – the one who has been the cause of these utter miseries – be very careful of them. Watch your step, my dear, do not give anyone any reason to side against you especially as you may not be able to rely on the support of your new friend – don't forget we now know he is the one who has twice failed to speak out when necessary. And, honey...they are saying do something about that pain."

Valerie had given Beth a great deal to think about after her surprise call. They would be talking again, that was a certainty and at last Beth did not feel weighed down by things she had been obliged to remember without getting closer to any rhyme or reason. She briefly pressed her abdomen where a pain had come and then set about the day's tasks. She had already been to her mother to make sure she had taken her pills correctly; pill taking had become a bit of a problem lately even though they were provided in a blister pack. All her mother had to do was open each section when required, take out the clutch of pills and swallow them but recently Beth had been finding a few on the floor or some sections not even taken. This would have presented no great problem had the pills not included blood thinning and heart medications. Time was coming when she would have to visit her mother maybe three times a day for pill taking, but for the moment her neighbour was happy to pop in at tea time and, for some reason, the bedtime pill was always remembered and taken without fail. So far.

Buzz buzz. Hi, B. How are things? Want to come over later? x J

Write message: Oh, lovely, yes please. 7:30? x B Press send.

Buzz buzz. Yes, 7:30 is good. x J

That would work out well. Charlotte would be home for her dinner at 6pm before going out again to George's house. They had been friends for years, since primary school days in fact, and now they were to be going their separate ways – Charlotte to Southampton and George to Nottingham. Not the end of the world, they would still manage to see each other from time to time and they could FaceTime or message. It was a given fact that they would always be in contact; they were as close as Daniel and Charlotte. Beth's thoughts went back to Valerie's words, 'Do something about that pain.' She decided that it was nothing that warranted action and set about getting dinner ready. What Beth hadn't reckoned on was being whacked until she took notice of Spirit and, as she absently stroked her abdomen again, she experienced the most agonising pain which made her scream. She instantly lay down and was surprised to feel something move before the pain went; that was enough to do it and she telephoned the surgery for an appointment. Spirit was really working on Beth's behalf because, much to her surprise, she was told there had been a cancellation at 4pm so if she could get there by then the appointment was hers. Dr. Gorgeous, as all the women called him, carried out the examination required, carefully read her notes and listened to the stories behind her scars. He was relatively new to the surgery and was just what they needed – he got things done – if he said a scan would be organised within a week, it was. He delivered the news that he was going to request an urgent appointment with a consultant as he considered that this should not be left too long, giving her a knowing look as he did so. Beth knew not to ask and, besides, she had her own suspicions, which at that particular moment she really didn't want to think about.

She decided not to tell James much about the visit to the GP because, well, there really wasn't anything to tell yet. All he needed to know was that she was being referred to a consultant about abdominal pains. As usual, when they met the sparks of connection began to fly and it wasn't long before they were sharing a kiss and a cuddle, which held the promise of further intimacy between them.

"Beth, are you sure you are OK with this? I don't want to...we shouldn't...because...oh, come here." James wrapped his arms around her in a hug which said, 'I so want to be close to you but don't want this to end up with you hurting.'

Beth's own arms went around his neck and they hugged tightly, their whole selves blending into one another like butter into toast. They drew apart and looked deeply into each other's eyes, both of them showing fear of what was happening yet with total understanding at the same time. In one small movement they connected and the electrifying moment of his lips touching hers sent her hand to the back of his head, pulling him closer to her. They kissed long, deep and strong, their tongues meeting and, as the frenzy of passion welled in them both, James lifted her bra and closed his mouth over her breast at first gently, oh so gently, flicking his tongue over the nipple as it hardened. The gasps from Beth were of pure want and need. James was lost in his own want as he sucked at her breasts until both he and Beth were breathless with furious passion; Beth's back arching to intensify the pleasure, her mind begging him not to stop. Her hand found his desire hard and straining against his jeans, so ready for taking in her warm, soft hand and as she slowly and rhythmically squeezed, the sound from James's throat belied a deep longing in him.

"Beth...Beth...no further," he whispered in gasps of impassioned breath. "I'm sorry...you said last time...I'm sorry, I didn't mean to..."

"It's all right," she breathed. "I promise...it'll be all right."

They both came to their senses long enough to agree before feeling the awkwardness of the moment. It was Beth who broke what tension there may have been by saying in a mock stern voice, "You're quite right...no trousers come off and certainly no knickers come off!"

This made James laugh and he asked in a teasing voice, "Are you sure? Are you really, really sure?"

The comedy was not lost on Beth and she carried on as she replaced her clothes. "Yes. Firstly, I am still a married woman. Secondly, you are still grieving for Laura, and thirdly, which should possibly be firstly, I am here to do a job for you, remember?"

James looked at her, raised one eyebrow, and said with a steady gaze, "I thought you were?"

They both fell about laughing as Beth giggled, "You know what I mean! I think you have been brought into my life for a specific purpose – I've just got to work out what that exact purpose is."

She decided it was time to tell him the whole story of Mark and how she'd been informed that she was in danger of uterine cancer at that time by Joe and Tina. She told of how ill she had become and how it actually culminated in her having a full hysterectomy. "The thing is, James, I think you may be another Mark and I have to take you somewhere and leave you there...or to put it another way, stay with you until I know where you have to go and then I must stand right back," she concluded.

James looked sad as he asked, "So what are we to do, B? I can't not hug you."

He was secretly very pleased with Beth's answer of, "And I can't not hug you either."

James was on a seesaw, "But look what happens when we do!"

Always close to herself, Beth gave nothing away as she said, "It'll be OK. I will step back when the time comes...when we discover what it is."

"Even if it is another woman? Are you sure?" asked James.

She managed to keep her voice even with, "I did it for Mark. What we had was intense; we might just as well have had an affair, so I'm sure I can."

"OK, but we must try to calm ourselves down, I think," said James, not fully convinced that they could.

Beth's smiling reply of "OK. Agreed," gave James no hint that she would have any difficulty in putting restraint into their meetings.

Beth and James had both underestimated what had happened that night. Over the next few weeks they spent many evenings behaving like teenagers, sharing fun, kisses, hugs, touches, even getting pretty close to losing control but sense always prevailing usually in the guise of comedy. It was unspoken between them but desire for the other was simmering just under the surface, each using humour to mask the underlying hurt, longing and need.

The appointment with the consultant was, indeed, carried out fairly hastily and on leaving the hospital Beth texted James to tell him that she was facing major surgery. His concern for her health was evident and he asked her to call round so he could glean everything there was to know – they talked and laughed for a long time. Friendly as they were, Beth never talked about herself much and certainly not about any of her achievements...something probably left over from childhood when she never felt part of anything and, in essence, invisible. The Beth who had feelings, ideas and opinions always kept to herself and rarely said what she really felt personally. In fact, she had learned at an early age to put herself down before anyone else could do so. Ridicule hurt, so why should she allow anyone to do it to her. If she said it, all the malice was gone, there was no sting, and it was a very good way of beating bullies and enemies. Yes, it had served her well over time...it had taught her how to let her face show no emotion. So when James said he was going to Hazel's later that day she smiled and kept the bruised feeling to herself. He didn't need to know what she felt and she told herself that thoughts of Charlotte away at university would override those feelings. Still, she couldn't help but initiate a deliberately probing conversation by telling him that in the past she had not fared well through surgical procedures even requiring a 5-pint blood transfusion at the last medical intervention.

"Tell you what James...if I get through it OK I'll text you. If I don't, the nurse will text you," her laughter making it sound like light-hearted banter.

His reaction was immediate. "Oh! Don't say that, please don't say that. You must live...you will live." James's face was deadly serious.

So, he did take her life seriously! Beth then put on her own serious head and let him know she was concerned that things may not work out as planned and would be writing letters to be delivered in the event of her death. They talked about many things including the similarities in their personality traits – for instance, when at a seminar or function of any kind neither of them would mix with the others at break times preferring, instead, to stay aloof. They spoke of similarities in their childhoods, their respective abdominal problems and their love of Marmite. The unfolding parallels in their lives were fascinating.

James could not fail to see it and he blurted out, "My God, Beth! We are the same!"

When she put it to him that they were a split soul he agreed that they were certainly from the same hive. This would explain why they were so comfy in each other's company and why so many people expected that where one of them was, so would be the other. Even so it hadn't registered with him that they were, in fact, true soulmates.

Everything was moving very fast regarding Beth's surgery and the procedure was carried out exceptionally quickly. As it turned out her fears became fact and she did not get through surgery well, having had to spend more than twice as long as expected under anaesthetic because it proved to be a complicated case, plus it was a struggle to stabilise her afterwards. Instead of being back on the ward within the anticipated two hours, Beth was not released from the Recovery Room for almost five. The first thing she did was to ask for her mobile phone and found two messages waiting:

Hi B. How are you feeling? J. 17:30

Hi B. Did you make it? J. 19:05

Realising that the last message was 40 minutes old she thought James may now be afraid of what he might hear if he rang the hospital, so she tapped out her reply as fast as her fragile state would allow:

Write message: Alive. Got back to ward 10mins ago. Not too well. B Press send. 19:55

Buzz buzz: Glad to hear you are there. You'll be all right...just rest now and let your body do the rest. Healing prayers for you. J x. 19:57

Write message: Thank you. Can't think very clearly. Spk 2mro. Very tired. Painful. B 20:30

Buzz buzz: Let them give you medication to help you sleep. You are not alone. Chin up. Hug. J. 21:24

Three days later Beth was sent home and James spent quite a lot of time with her, took her out and generally was very attentive and caring. He cared, that much was obvious.

Hazel was not at all happy that James had been talking to Beth. She wanted to be the only woman he took notice of, so what could she do to make herself that woman? So far he had fallen into line with her actions nicely but now he was talking to HER again. She had seen him walking around Waitrose with her, chatting, laughing and even sharing a trolley with her. This was not on and she had to do something to make herself more special to James and keep him away from HER. The thing was, as Hazel very well knew, James was the one who sought Beth out far more than the other way round. This would not do...something had to change.

CHAPTER TWELVE

Every time it was Holly's weekend to stay with her dad she was keen to see Beth. They got along very well together and there was a genuine affection between them. When they were together James was relaxed, Holly was happy and it pleased Beth to see them like this. The shadows of Laura's absence took a back seat for a while and Holly could be the carefree 10-year-old she should be and her dad could feel real pleasure in watching her flourish. Ray and June were doing a marvellous job with their granddaughter but even they couldn't bring out the Holly who could put her grief aside completely; the memories of her mum were too great at her grandparents' house even though Ray and June had worked through their own grief. Their only concern now was Holly and her wellbeing, and James's state of mind. At times he was definitely not resigned to being a widower and struggled to cope. Ray would sometimes find him sitting under a tree in the corner of their garden, looking completely lost, unable to comprehend how life had brought them all to this point. James didn't cry very often now but Ray knew the look in his face was a representation of the despair of the loss he still felt...they all still felt. Laura should still be there with them – she was too young to be taken so cruelly; a life not lived out; all her expectations and hopes stopped in their tracks and unrealised. She would never see her daughter blossom into a young woman, never see her get married or have children of her own. Life was so unfair – it gave the wondrous joy of the birth of a child yet without warning would take a life away again with no regard for age. Both Ray and June had noticed a change in Holly recently. Something had somehow started to de-demonise the concept of death. She had brought a book back from her dad's a couple of weeks or so ago, telling her grandparents that Beth had introduced her to the stories of Terry Pratchett. A little concerned at the artistry on the book sleeve they waited until Holly had gone to school one day and then very carefully borrowed the book to read some of the story themselves. To their astonishment they found the story hilarious and began to understand the shift in Holly's outlook. *Soul Music* was, indeed, a jolly good read. The relationship between them all was good and strong so it was hardly surprising that Ray and June felt as if they'd violated Holly's trust and love and it was not difficult for them to tell her what they had done and why. Rather than be angry, which June felt Holly was quite entitled to be, she laughed and asked if her gran would read her a chapter or two when she went to bed. From then on a new way of life took form. Ray bought the Terry Pratchett books for them all to enjoy – *Mort*, *Going Postal*, *The Hogfather*, *Interesting Times*, *Feet of Clay*, *Men At Arms*, *Thief of Time*, *Witches Abroad* and more. Over time they enjoyed every single one of them.

Changes in James were widely being noticed and they were not good. He was not the man he used to be. He was becoming less caring, selfish, not noticing when he was being hurtful and everyone could see who was behind these changes. The day came when the bombshell Beth had dreaded was delivered by James when he told her that he wasn't being fair to Hazel and that he had confessed to her about Beth...not all the details, just that he had allowed himself to become a bit too close...and he was not going to be able to see Beth on the same basis any more. At least he'd had the decency to say it to her face but it cut her to the core, even though she knew she had to let him go one day. She didn't make a fuss, she didn't cry – not in his presence – she just walked away thinking that that was the end of something she knew she would miss forever. There would be a huge void in her life but she had to move on, get out of that situation and not allow her emotions to dictate to her. She had enough else on her plate, why should she waste time on the dreadful way James had treated her? Could it have been her own fault? She shouldn't have let it develop...but how do you stop something developing when you don't even realise what exactly has started? It had been less than 48 hours when her mobile phone came to life.

Buzz buzz. I'm so sorry...for everything. J

A sudden and hard pain hit Beth's chest as those first three words resounded in her head relentlessly and thoughts...no!...memories, flashed by – and in a second she knew for sure. I'M SO SORRY...I'M SO SORRY...I'M SO SORRY...I'M SO SORRY. Her heart was ready to burst and she wanted to howl and scream until there was not a single breath left to be had. Right then, at that moment, she wanted to be relieved of this life, to be taken away so as not to have to experience the pain and utter torment. The word 'wretched' came nowhere close to how she felt. As she sobbed, the one previous life story she had not yet told anyone played out in her memory, twisting the invisible knife in her heart with every syllable and image.

The dream had given her two different scenes, which made up the whole sad and sorry tale. A boy, again aged about 10 or 12, with blond curly hair and dressed in a dark blue, brass-buttoned jacket which stopped at waist level and white trousers, stood on the deck of an old ship – the sort powered only by sails – and there, in front of him was the barrel of rum. As with the other dreams, the silent knowledge was there...this was the 1600s and he was a cabin boy. The young boy was looking towards land as though he was missing his home and whoever lived there. Then came the voice – 'I'm so sorry' – and now there was no doubt at all as to whose voice it was. How could she have been so slow to recognise it? All those years ago when she'd had that dream – getting on for 20 years Beth thought – it had had no meaning and now she had to face it, she knew full well whose voice it was...there was no hiding from it any longer.

The second part of the dream was of a tavern, a well kept place, where a young woman stood with strawberry blonde hair tumbling in loose natural curls to her shoulders. She wore a white mop cap, long brown dress with criss-crossed bodice, a white under-blouse with the puffed sleeves caught in at the elbow and flaring out below, and a full-skirted white apron. She stood with one hand on the doorjamb as she looked earnestly out at the horizon. She was waiting for someone, or looking for someone. I'M SO SORRY...I'M SO SORRY... The setting screamed 1600s. The knowledge was that the tavern girl was Beth's soul, the boy on the ship was her son but it wasn't clear if The Voice, the unseen man with a lovely, soft, educated voice, was the father. The ship went down and the boy lost his life. The status of the relationship between

The Voice and the tavern girl was not directly given yet it filtered through that it was a loving relationship but their union would have been prohibited...she had been too low born for that...and he had been kept away from her, even when she needed him most. So she had lost her son and her lover. Beth had often wondered about how the boy came to be on the ship in the first place and thought it most probable that The Voice had bought the boy a place thus giving him a good start in life and guaranteeing him a decent life ahead.

James had now been disclosed as The Voice, indisputably so. The knowledge clanged in as loudly as an iron door slams shut and Beth ached with pain in every sinew and bone, with every breath and beat of her heart, and with every thought she had. This life was becoming too much to bear; if there was a God surely he, she or it, would not allow such pain and grief. The level of grief was astounding; the grief, all of the griefs she bore, were not only a present day thing, it was centuries old. It had been carried, unresolved, and brought forward to now and it was all coming out together. How was she supposed to survive this? What Beth hadn't reckoned on was fate stepping in with a slight helping hand. The sound of her iPad announcing an incoming FaceTime call gave her something else to think about and she was delighted, although her face showed nothing but misery, to see it was Valerie calling from Canada.

"Hi, Honey. How are you? Something told me you are in very great need. What's happening?" she asked and Valerie listened intently as Beth explained everything to her. They had a long chat during which Valerie read her a verse which started, 'God would not have given you the darkness if he thought you could have taken the light.' They talked about the connotations of the whole verse but for today they decided that Beth was ready for 'the light,' this time meaning the final understanding of previous lives and relationships and this was why all these people – Mark, her parents, James, Hazel – were here together in this lifetime. She was now in the light of truth and she was in the position of being able to reconcile the many facets or aspects of the lives represented by everyone around her. In theory. Theory was good but it was still only theory. How was she to find the practical side of it? She didn't want to play – this was too hard and she didn't know what to do or which way to turn.

"Oh, V...why can't it all just end?" asked a very weary-spirited Beth. "And where are all my graves? I must have graves all over the place...I'd love to know where they are," she finished with not a hint of disguising the frustration in her voice, but at least she laughed at the thought of wanting to find her graves. Of all the things she could have wanted to do, she wanted to find her graves! There wasn't much chance of that happening...but, wait! When was her last lifetime?

Probably early 1800s...there may be a possibility of finding that one, if only she knew who she'd been and where she'd lived. Perhaps she would indulge in another regression and see if it bore fruit. What an exciting thought and even as she was thinking, it became a rolling stone quickly gaining momentum.

Contact with James didn't quite stop...she wouldn't hear from him for many days at a time when she would then receive a message saying, "Hi B. How are you?" or "Hi B. it's been ages...I miss our conversations." Then it would be, "Hi B. Would you like to come and see Holly? She would like to see you." Her replies were always economic and non-committal but the number of messages he sent within a couple of months made Beth wonder if he was truly happy with Hazel. Eventually she went to see Holly and when James asked her to stay a while after Holly had gone to bed so that they could talk, it soon became clear that the magic between the two of them was far from gone. They laughed until their sides hurt, they hugged every time they were close to each other, and they danced a waltz around the room. When they shared a deep embrace their passions inflamed and neither could think of anything but the person they were holding; the strength of the emotion overtook them. Beth could feel James's heart pounding against her, an electric charge seemed to flash through her body hardening her nipples in frenzied anticipation and with an unconscious move he took her hand and placed it on the most intimate part of his body. It felt so natural to have her holding and exciting him, the throb of his pulse making him hard, very hard. When Beth held his gaze with questioning eyes he replied with equally questioning lips, kissing her gently and tenderly – the kiss asking if he may continue. It was as though they were both sucked up in a whirlwind as the surroundings vanished and they spiralled in a frenzy of ecstasy, exploring each other in ways so far forbidden. Beth was barely aware, and yet blissfully aware, of his hand caressing her femininity and as she rocked to the motion of its movement and her overwhelming desire, his fingers slid into her warmth, bringing groans of sheer need from both of them. His hardness pulsated in response to Beth's soft hand pleasuring him and the thrusting of his fingers into her body took her to an intoxicating state of passion she had never known before; they were oblivious to the world, registering only the desperate desire so stirred within them both. The crescendo to the lovemaking which came so naturally was almost upon them, the moment of consummation just a whisper away, their breathing fast and furious, each unable to get enough of the other. Each wanted so desperately for the culmination of their bodies at last joining together in unbridled sex but both gathered every ounce of willpower to withdraw from the beautiful liaison that seemed so right and yet so wrong, leaving them both consumed with the unspoken frustration of unfulfilled sexual tension.

The following week was a little strained between them until eventually James said he didn't know what he was going to tell Hazel...that he shouldn't do it to her. It knocked Beth off balance. How could he do it to Hazel? How could he do it to HER? Had it meant nothing to him? Obviously not, so she kept her own counsel and said nothing to argue against his statement...after all, she had promised him she would let him go. Oh, Lord! This hurt. What hurt her even more was when he sent a simple text to say he had confessed to Hazel, that they were getting back on track and he had to make some changes. She knew exactly what those changes would be...and they didn't include her. Her head spun as the word 'confessed' crashed round and round – he had done it again! Whenever Beth hit a certain level of emotional pain she busied herself with moving furniture or arranging all her cupboards. This time it was the volumes of photographs she decided to sort out and she began to organise them into chronological order. They were already vaguely in some order in that they were in bundles of her as a child, of wedding pictures, of Daniel and Charlotte at all ages, of friends and so on. About an hour into her distraction tactics she stopped abruptly as she picked up one photo, her eyes glued to the faces looking back at her. She reached for the telephone and rang Frankie. Beth made two cups of tea, opened a packet of heavily coated chocolate biscuits and sat at the table waiting for the doorbell to ring. It only took Frankie ten minutes to get to Beth's house and she couldn't wait to find out what it was that had her friend in such a stew.

"What do you see in this picture, Frankie?" Beth asked. "This was taken on my last day at work when I was heavily pregnant with Charlotte."

Frankie looked at all the faces and then her jaw dropped. She looked at Beth, back at the picture and declared, "My God, Beth! You look like James! This is uncanny."

Beth said nothing; her emotions completely shot again, her eyes glassy with hovering tears. Frankie listened to how stupid Beth was feeling and why she was diverting her attention by turning out the photographs and then, in the unprompted way of a friend, went into the kitchen and came back with two glasses, bottles of wine, nuts, crisps and a box of tissues – just in case. They sat silently, nibbling and drinking until the first glass of wine had been consumed and the conversation resumed.

"I can't believe you and James look so similar," said Frankie. "Everyone knows that you two are like bangers and mash – where one is we expect to see the other. It is almost like you are twins, or joined at the hip...or something."

Beth had poured them each another glass of wine and as she picked hers up she said to Frankie, "I had a very interesting conversation with Jo the other day when, oddly enough, she said pretty much the same thing, but she added a few other things which got me thinking. Now that this photograph has surfaced it has made me sit up and take notice. Jo was saying about how she was supposed to have been a twin it seems; her mother was pregnant, miscarried, but then went on to have a baby. This can only mean that she miscarried one baby, in which case, Jo had been a twin. She thinks this is why she is so nervy and has a tendency to say things twice...because she hasn't got the back-up of the twin...she is somehow only half of what she is meant to be."

Frankie listened intently as her friend continued, "I have always felt like something is missing or I am 'out on a limb'. Suppose I was one of a twin? Mother told me years ago that she had been informed she had miscarried yet I was born at the due time, so it is not outside the realms of possibility that she was carrying twins and only one of us survived. And isn't it odd that when I do the food shopping I almost always buy two of everything? I mean, what's that all about? Why?"

They both mused over everything said and more besides, including reincarnation. They picked at the crisps and nuts and Beth let Frankie think about it a bit longer – a good call because it wasn't long before she asked, "I know James is a few years younger than you, but am I being daft in thinking that James could have been your twin? This is why you are so alike in many ways, why you get on so well, and now, with this photograph?"

Beth smiled, thankful that her friend had seen what she was suspecting herself. It was too easy to arrive at an idea like that when it involved yourself, but if someone else was to come up with it then that put a face of reality on it, albeit a small face. "That had crossed my mind," she answered. "Plus, think on this. I have had loads of abdominal troubles, haven't I? Well, so has James and apart from not having absolutely identical problems the difference is that mine have been corrected by surgery but his are ongoing and may even turn into something dreadful later on. What if he came with me as a twin and absorbed the worst of the problems – maybe as an apology for all the things he did in past lives – and then he took himself back to spirit?" Beth closed her eyes in silence for the few seconds it took her to acknowledge and dread the thought that, indeed, he had taken the worst of the abdominal problems by way of apology; to compound it he was even going to stay with Hazel so that she was the one who had to suffer watching him succumb to the ravages of the possible fatal illnesses they could mutate into, again saving Beth from further desperate pain. Shaking the thought away she continued, "Looking at another angle, Jo also reminded me that I'd once told her that I spoke a little but enough to be understood at 6 months old and I walked at 9 months old. She asked if I had been in a hurry to get here and then when I mentioned how much vocabulary I could understand before the age of 18 months she then asked, jokingly, if I had been 'erased' properly before coming in as a baby, because it is believed that a spirit is relieved of all knowledge before being reborn on to the earth plane." She continued, "I think she was right. As my tinker dad and biological dad of centuries ago had got together in this lifetime, in order for me to sort out that past life I had to be born when I was because of their ages...I think I was destined to meet James later on but I had to come too early. That could be a present day shot from the tinker dad – as my mother – still stopping me from going where I was meant to go, just as he stopped Rose from finding her real father. And," she finished, "that theory would explain the looks, the closeness, the similarities and the parallels in our lives that keep showing up in my tarot readings. Every single reading I have had includes either parallels or part readings which are for, or relate to, James, and why I know so much about the past lives – you know, the unspoken knowledge that came in so often. Bizarre, or what?"

They drained their glasses and poured another drink, both ready for it and neither feeling the slightest bit squiffy. They sat in silence whilst Beth's words settled in their respective consciousness.

Frankie was the first to speak. With a depth of seriousness rarely shown she said, "No, not bizarre. I think you are right, or pretty near right. I can't even pretend to be anywhere near your level of understanding of these matters but my heart and my head are yelling at me to accept it as truth. Beth, I am here to help you, if I can, with the pain or joy of all your lives. For this life in particular my dearest wish for you, my dear friend, is that you and James reach a happy conclusion to your reasons for knowing each other now." After she had given Beth a hug of encouragement she raised her glass to her friend in a silent toast, and drank the lot. Five minutes later she was asleep on Beth's couch.

Beth covered Frankie with a blanket and sat. Just sat. "...with the pain or joy of all your lives...," she recalled Frankie saying. "...with the pain or joy of all your lives...."

It struck Beth like a thunderbolt. All her past life dreams had a common thread and the moment she realised what it was unbidden tears streaked her cheeks. That common thread was enforced separation. The pair by the choppy seas, separated by disaster; the Chinese man, separated by unnatural death; the boy in the gladiatorial arena, by scheming and unnatural death; the monk, again scheming and unnatural death; the girl raised by the tinkers, stolen from her parents; the tavern girl and the boy on the ship, separated by unnatural death and scheming; the soldier, separated by death in battle. Spirit was working with Beth and the unspoken knowledge that now passed into her was knocking her sideways. It had taken her a while to get used to knowing that her mum and dad had been the tinker and natural father, just as it had when she realised that Mark had been the one at the harbour and again the soldier. Right now she had to come to grips with the new knowledge of the players in the lifetimes of the gladiatorial ring, the monk, and the tavern girl and boy on the ship. It had been so glaringly obvious, probably so much so that it could not be seen. Goddammit! The king had even been shown to her as James and the queen as Hazel...the hair and face of James, and the mannerisms and stance of Hazel. The monk had been herself, the jester had been Hazel and the voice had been James. As for the tavern girl, well, she always knew that was her spirit but she had not, until now, matched the voice saying 'sorry' to that of James. Hazel's involvement in this one was in keeping the tavern girl and 'the voice' apart. The worst thing was realising that the same triangle of people were locked again into battle. The two boys appeared in Beth's mind, standing side by side, and she realised that the souls of this pair of brave boys had come back to her as Daniel and Charlotte, of that there was now no question. Beth and James had found each other again for the purpose of sorting themselves out, but the ever jealous spirit of Hazel had pushed her way in again to stop them and Beth knew, without any shadow of doubt, that she would do anything and everything possible to do so. Beth picked up pen and paper and began to write:

The harbour. Number of people: 3. Who? Me (woman/hooded character) and Mark (crocodile head) and "Darth Vader". Result for me: grief.

Chinese man. Number of people: 2. Who? Daniel (poor man), emperor (baby Adam) Result for me: Tricky... Death of Adam (who was part of me) followed by grief.

Ancona. Number of people: 4. Who? James (king), Hazel (queen), me (child's mother), child (Daniel). Result for me: grief.

Monk. Number of people: 3. Who? Me (monk), Hazel (jester), James (voice). Result for me: death.

Tinkers. Number of people: 3. Who? Mum (tinker), brother (tinker's son), me (girl). Result for me: death. Running girl. Number of people: 2. Who? Me (girl), dad (man in house). Result for me: grief.

Tavern girl. Number of people: 4. Who? Boy (Charlotte), me (tavern girl & boy's mother), James (the voice), (and

Hazel, although not seen in dream prevented "James" from seeing girl/me again). Result for me: grief.

Soldier. Number of people: 2. Who? Mark (soldier), me (lady in blue). Result for me: grief.

What reason was there for her to even consider that this life should produce anything other than a result of grief or death? Only that she seemed to be sorting her lives out one by one this time round. She had happily resolved her dad; that with her mother was not yet over; the one with Mark had a happy ending in that he was now his own man and her health had been rescued; she understood why baby Adam wasn't to live and her mind was at rest. That left James and Hazel. She just couldn't see that one having a happy ending for her. Beth cleared away the evidence of their "girls' night in," wrapped the second blanket around herself and slept in her recliner chair beside her comatose friend.

CHAPTER THIRTEEN

Right now Beth loathed James. She hated him for what he had done, hated him for how he had treated her and hated him for how she now felt. He had chosen Hazel to be his girlfriend yet he still treated Beth with the same degree of behaviour as ever. Times he had agreed that they must only be friends and there would be no more intimacy between them and all had been well – until he moved the goalposts again and had resumed the behaviour of someone much more than a friend. Times he had said he had to look at himself in the mirror and he had to be fair to Hazel. The last time he had said, "It would devastate her, crush her, and I can't do that – she is a nice person, isn't she?" To which Beth simply answered, "So am I," and buried her hurt. She realised that she never initiated anything which could have led to him running his hands all over her or cuddling her, or any of the other lovely things he did, but neither did she stop him. It was always spontaneous and genuine. No-one could behave like that for self-satisfaction and then feel so guilty. Now he had misbehaved again, confessed to Hazel and Beth was being dealt the punishment. He had not contacted her, nor had he answered Beth's question, "Am I to keep away from you and not contact you again?" save to say, "We'll talk about that." And then a few days later came, "Just wanted to say thank you for all the brilliant things you have said and done and all the help you have given." To which Beth replied, "I'm guessing that is the precursor to saying you are throwing me away." That was the last message between them and Beth had assumed she was right. God, it hurt. Then he had sought her out in the library where he knew she would be; Holly was with him and the meeting was tense to say the very least. James asked Beth if she would join them at home for a cup of tea and she only accepted because he asked four times and Holly said she would really like her to.

"I'm not supposed to be here am I?" Beth asked James as he passed her a cup of tea.

"Well, no, I suppose you're not," he said. "...But...ohhhh, this is not right! It's all wrong! The world is wrong...I...you..."

"Then I shall go. Thank you for making the tea...sorry I shan't be drinking it," Beth said as she tried to push her chair back to stand up.

"No, don't go...stay," he said. But he kept looking at his watch and out of the window every time he heard a vehicle; obviously worried that Hazel would turn up and find her there.

"You haven't texted and you haven't answered my questions...I'm scared to death to text you because it will get you into trouble...what am I supposed to do?" Beth hurriedly asked.

"What questions?" James asked. "Oh!...yes... I must answer you, I will text...I will text you...there's lots of things I haven't done lately and getting into trouble for it...I haven't put in some paperwork at work, reports I haven't done and people I should have spoken to...including you..." A message arrived on his mobile and he had to tell Beth that Hazel was on her way and, knowing it would only take her about five minutes, Beth pushed her mug away and said she would go. She was sorry she had to leave the tea and made her way to the door leaving James looking beaten and dejected.

"There is one thing I would say," continued Beth. "At no time in any of this was it ever considered that I might have feelings to consider." As soon as she'd said this she metaphorically kicked herself for using the words 'considered' and 'consider' in the same short sentence.

James hung his head and began to stutter – something Beth had never heard him do before – "Of course, of...of course you...you h-have feelings, of course you have feelings...I will text...text you...I will text you."

And even as he was still speaking Beth said one word – "Bye." She walked out of the door and away from his house without a backward glance. She was shaking because she knew how close she was to running into Hazel – the last thing she wanted to do – and yet she was hoping that Hazel would see her walking away from his house.

Three days later he still hadn't contacted her and she wondered if Hazel was making herself omnipresent – perhaps she found out that Beth had been at the house and was making his life difficult. He had a lot of work to do for the college so he wouldn't be needing that from her. Tough. She hated what he had done to her. Hated him. Hated Hazel. Hated herself.

Beth felt as though she was in a complete vacuum of nothingness and there was nowhere to go, nothing she could do to end it, no-one who could help and nowhere else her mind or emotions could turn. Everything was at a standstill, yet the circle of it all kept turning with no hope of breaking; even when a possible way through presented itself somehow it just added to the circle of nothingness. One answer depended on another which depended on another which, in turn, depended on yet another, yet no one thing could be answered without adding to the negativity of another. It was rather like being allergic to water, Beth thought wryly. She had all this information which could help someone she cared for very much from making the mistake of his life, but there was no way he would listen and, even if he did, how likely was it that he would believe what she told him? The short answer was 'not a chance, not even a remote chance'. Then again, it was all quite remarkable stuff from an unprovable source so she couldn't expect him to listen. But she knew, without a shadow of doubt, that it was all true. James had already been to the Spiritualist Church with her and was accepting of everything it had to offer so that was a start, but dreamwork? Could she expect him to embrace that? She and James had enjoyed each other's company very much from the moment they met and many people thought, and still did, that they were a couple and they possibly could have been had Hazel not set her cap at him. Beth had not pushed herself forward in his life although she hoped he would continue the lovely easy-going relationship they had, whatever it was. He was not averse to cuddling her, saying how he missed her, spending time with her, taking her to dinner, and having glorious evenings of adult horseplay. He often declared that he'd told Hazel she was a giant pain in the arse and not the type of person he wanted. Nevertheless, she would up her game every time and worm her way back into his life and it was clear from the things James said that she had manipulated him into doing what she wanted. She had this knack of giving him two or three disguised choices of a course of action yet, whichever one he chose, it would bring him to the same conclusion – and he couldn't see it. Hazel was not a well liked person in the village and no matter who James asked about her nature, he always got the same reply...not always wrapped in cotton wool...and it was always to say that she was manipulative, controlling and, by her own admission, would keep up any pretence until she got what she wanted no matter how long it took. It was as though she had some hold over him and he did not dare go against her. Beth had always felt that Hazel was systematically getting to James so that he would have nothing more to do with her, not even speak to her, and it had finally happened.

Beth needed to get away. Away from the house, the village, everyone and, more importantly, herself. She was turning herself inside out with emotion, thought and memories – some far more distant than others; she felt as though her heart was breaking. Again! There was only one thing she could do immediately and that was to walk and walk and walk, and try to clear her mind as she went. To be out with nature and the elements, all God's artistry, may just bring some kind of clarity and if not, well, she would come home, sob her heart out for as long as she wanted behind closed doors.

So, wearing her most comfortable shoes, umbrella in hand and her switched off mobile in her pocket together with a little money, Beth took herself off for a very long walk. She had no idea where she would go or how long it would take. It really didn't matter. There was nothing to go home for, no-one who needed her to be anywhere, no-one waiting for her. The one thing she had at last admitted to herself was that she wanted, needed, the love of a good man; someone to share her love with. The love within her felt empty; oh, she loved her children immeasurably, she loved her friends, but she still felt empty. What a dreadful realisation, that although she loved all these people she still felt empty. Giving love is one of those unconditional things and should be enough. Ha! Should! Ought! Words of control, instruction, dictatorial words. Why SHOULD it be enough? Why not say CAN be enough, or MIGHT be enough, MAY be enough?

As she walked thoughts crowded her mind, all looking for an answer there and then, and every thought seemed to have one word in it. James. Why could she not shift him from her mind? They had never totally given in to the sexual attraction between them, and certainly never taken anything to the bedroom – they'd both agreed about that in the beginning although on many occasions they could have easily given in to desire and very nearly did; and then there was Hazel. It was so very hurtful that he could just pick Beth up and put her down, and so many times. "So help me, God," she said softly into the morning air. "I've let him walk right into my heart, but why, when he treats me like this? When did that happen?" And she thought more about some of the messages she'd received from him. "I owe it to you..." And she'd replied, "You owe me nothing," because to know he'd done something he regarded as a debt rather than a promise he'd made took away the warmth of the promise. It turned it into something he felt he had to do for her and that was not a pleasant thought. Actually, yes, he did owe her a great deal. He owed her three lifetimes of debt. He owed the maidservant, he owed the monk and he owed the tavern girl. How could he have sent his own son into the gladiatorial arena to his certain death? Had he not a single thought for the boy or the maid? He had not had the courage to speak out to make the truth known which would have saved the monk from the noose. Not had the courage because...why? Was he not willing to take the consequences? The image of the jester as the monk met his fate pervaded Beth's mind and made her shudder. As for the tavern girl who lost the boy on the ship and her lover at the same time...the pain she endured was unimaginable. Again, he'd not been strong enough to stand up for what was right. She fully recognised the players in all of these scenes, James being the king and the two voices. She knew her soul was that of the maid, the monk and the tavern girl so she inwardly acknowledged that James did owe her after all, but he didn't owe Beth – he owed her soul. Was that the purpose of them being brought together now? For him to make right all that had been so wrong before? If he were to give himself to her spirit would it resolve? But he didn't want her. Round and round her thoughts went. Why does he keep going back to Hazel when she constantly angers him, controls him and is so dominant? Hazel was obviously the manifestation of the souls of the queen, the jester and whoever took him away from the girl at the tavern. She had always had the control. Has he no backbone? Was that Beth's job – to give him a backbone?

She thought of the night so recently when James had invited her over for the evening, as often he did, and told her he was seeing Hazel again even though he had stated just a week before that she would have to really look at herself before he took her back. Thor's hammer could not have dealt a greater blow than the impact of the words he had just delivered and she had fallen all but silent. Beth didn't want to tell him what she thought of Hazel's manipulative behaviour or his decision. And she would not sink to speaking out in such a way. James, because he was male and couldn't see beyond the end of his nose, thought Charlotte's absence was making Beth sad; she didn't correct him, but eventually he said, "Have I done something wrong?"

Without hesitation she replied, "I don't know...have you?"

After a short while he asked if she would like to tell him what was on her mind.

With difficulty she eventually controlled her voice and face to say, "I sometimes wish I had never met you; I'm glad I did, but can't help but think it might have been better if I hadn't."

His recovery was, "If you hadn't you would not have met Holly, or Ray and June, and you wouldn't have had the happiness you found."

Trying to curtail the rising frustration within she fired back, "No, I would not have, but at least I would have remained in blissful ignorance of what my life was."

Beth was hurt, very hurt. A fourth life of hurt, all at the hands of the same two people – just as Valerie had warned.

So just how was this lifetime going to work out? Looking at what the centuries had to tell, it would seem that this lifetime was the one where he would take her as his own at last. But if he wasn't going to love her, what was this lifetime all about? Why was he here, why were they all here together? How can it possibly work out anywhere near right with karmic balance and so on?

"Sacred Spirit, Angels of Light, Guides and Guardians – and dad – please let me hear or see how this is all going to end without me being symbolically slapped across the face by either James or Hazel. I'm tired of crying, of breaking my heart. How can my heart be mended after all these centuries of hurt? How is he supposed to make it up to me? Surely the answer has to be that we are meant to be together this time, especially as I'm not coming back again. Surely karma won't let me lose again? Please let me hear or see."

Beth was not really surprised to find that the words she spoke into the ether were accompanied by tears, many, many tears.

What happened next was almost an immediate reply to her plea as her second, and last, regression flashed before her eyes. At the time she had not fully understood it and there did not seem to be any story to it. Jools had tried her best during the session but it had taken an unexpected turn and decided to bring Beth out of it instead of continuing.

Jools, the owner of the holistic therapy business in town, was a gentle, happy and artistic lady in her early 40s who Beth had met about nine years ago when she joined the healing course Jools was running. They had become friends and the trust between them was mutually strong so it was an easy decision for Jools to carry out Beth's regression this time.

"Imagine yourself safe in a pure white light," Beth was instructed. "A soft pure white light of protection. This pure white light is all around you; you are totally protected. Now, look around you – what do you see? Where are you? Take note of what you are wearing."

"I can't see anything," came a doleful reply from Beth.

"Look at the walls, or anything around you. Can you see a door, perhaps?" asked Jools.

Beth was already beginning to feel uneasy and did her best to answer with something useful but could only say, "I can't see anything... the sides are a rough texture and very dark. There might be a door there but I can't see a handle. I can't move."

Jools' encouraging voice asked her several times to walk forward, sideways, or to turn around to see what was behind her and each time the answer was the same.

"I can't," and finally it was revealed that Beth was, she thought, lying or sitting down.

"I need you to stand up and move to a door."

"I can't...I think I am buried." By now Beth was beginning to feel agitated.

"It is OK Beth, there is someone with you...we all have guides with us and around us...yours will be there...can you see them?"

"There is something very big here. I don't know what it is but it looks like a massive Hagrid character." She went on to describe someone about 8ft tall and 5ft wide, no discernible face as it was covered in the bushiest brown eyebrows ever known and equally bushy hair, beard and moustache. He, and it was a he according to the now familiar silent knowledge, was completely brown, even his clothes were brown, yet he carried a pink sword. "His name is Yonas," Beth finished.

"OK, Yonas is there for your protection. He will help you. What is happening now?"

"I am lying down I think and can't move, but now I can see a chink of light through slightly open eyelids. I'm being buried alive...he has a shovel...my eyes are closing." Then Beth's visual perspective changed and The Oaf's face was suddenly close to her and his eyes were the prominent, and urgent, feature. From one brief look which didn't belong to its time she received messages of helplessness, terror, distress and the most earnest of apologies. The emotional clout of the scene was disturbingly difficult to understand.

Just a split second had passed when Jools said, "I am bringing you back now, Beth – 5...4...3...2...1...you are back in the room with me – take your time and open your eyes when you are ready."

Beth lay still on the couch and tried to gather details of what she had seen which, she decided, would have to be played down and not allowed to become something which could rule her mind. It was a horrid experience leaving her feeling hated, frightened, vulnerable yet protected and adored at the same time.

Jools ran through the notes she had made of the session and Beth filled in little bits which she had felt, heard or seen.

They weren't little bits at all but Beth delivered them as exciting, incidental revelations, giving a stellar performance conveying that she felt nothing short of happy fascination with them. She knew this was for her own benefit because if she allowed her true feelings room in her head she would end up in a place that she really didn't want to go. Jools heard Beth's version of the whole story of what those dying eyes saw.

Beth's persona had been male but she could not see what clothes were being worn. The confusion of whether she or he was lying down or sitting was because it wasn't a properly dug grave, and she knew it was a grave because of the angle at which The Oaf with his shovel and the mound of earth still waiting to be cast in appeared. She saw The Oaf's round face and stubble-covered head; the humped and bent-over back as the shovel was thrust into the soil for loading. She heard the incomprehensible anguished moans coming from the dungeons of this deeply tormented soul whose muffled ears starved him of their purpose, thus exposing him to a soundless world and making him the target for the most cruel of abuses from almost everyone. In her recount to Jools not once did she mention The Oaf's eyes. Why did it bother her so much?

As unhappiness wrapped itself around Beth again, thanks to James, the regression revealing The Oaf rumbled repeatedly around her head asking to be heard. More like begging to be understood, she thought. What did she need to understand? The last thing she had seen was his eyes and – those were not the eyes of someone regarded as an imbecile and she now recognised them instantly. The Oaf's eyes...James's eyes! She recognised it as another time when his soul had not defended hers when, at the behest of another, unidentified but not difficult to guess who, he had hurt her. It was the messages given by the eyes that troubled her in some way. Eyes don't lie...you cannot get away from the truth of eyes... they are the windows of the soul. Beth realised they were not for the man being buried, they were for her, and were from the only part of The Oaf which found a way to communicate; his soul. A dart of excitement pierced her analytical mind when she realised what that meant. The Oaf had been communicating with the future and she with the past at the same time. Parallel worlds! She had never been convinced of the parallel world theory but it was something she was going to be seriously considering from now on.

But maybe nothing had changed over the centuries. Beth never complained out loud when being upset by James or Hazel. Just as the maid had no voice, the monk had no voice, The Oaf had no voice and the wench had no voice. And just as others in each life had called the shots, so it was again. James did everything Hazel said; he didn't have the mettle to say no to her controlling ways. So he'd hurt Beth because she never complained and because he wouldn't face Hazel's tantrums. WAKE UP JAMES Beth thought.

As the miles disappeared under her feet Beth's feelings ranged from despair and sorrow to love and compassion and, eventually, to hurt and anger.

"He'll just have to put up with it then," she thought. "I'm not doing it any more. If he won't do anything about it himself then he has only himself to blame for his misery. But he deserves so much more...he is such a gentle man...Laura must have been a lovely person. Is he punishing himself because he was away on the day she died? I bet he is! Because he let her down and didn't tell her he loved her that fateful day he is now punishing himself by not allowing himself to be given soft love again. Poor guy. Silly man; stupid man. Wake up! Look at what you are doing. Would Laura want that?" Perhaps that was it. He was now taking the punishment for his previous inactions so was this the three punishments for the three lifetimes? Laura dying, putting up with Hazel and rejecting Beth?

Which brought her to thinking: "No, that's not quite right. That is only one punishment; losing what was perfect with Laura, the controlling influence of Hazel taking him over, and not taking the chance to atone for past transgressions with my soul. Where's my justification? Am I really to be left like this with nothing resolved for my soul? That doesn't feel right. It is a complete replay of what has been before."

As she gazed across the valley and saw the sun reflected by windows of houses miles away more thoughts came. "So where is the light for me? What is it? The sun's light is being reflected to me. Stars...I love starlight...that is reflected to me and scientifically speaking that is light years old, just like all this in my head is centuries old... Why am I here? Why is James here? Am I here for him, or is he here for me? What has he done for me except eventually hurt me all over again? Oh, Lord! He has brought memories. He was the last piece of the enormous jigsaw that is my life. Memories that I can make my book of. Reflection. Is this the only way he can help me? Bringing me all the material needed for my book? Without him coming into my life I would have never known who that last piece was and the rest of it would never have fallen into place. Is it going to be published? Might it be worth printing? Might it bring something useful if not for me, then for others? To earn money from it is all very well, but it is not what fills an empty heart. How is my heart to recover?"

All this seemed to answer some of Beth's questions but then brought a whole load more. Perhaps just to get it all down on paper, printed and put out in the public domain was to be her voice. She would at last have her voice. James had given her a voice which would tell the world about his weaknesses; he was going to be his own judge and jury; admitting and letting the world know of his failings; this was his ultimate punishment.

If his soul was ready to accept it that is all very well, thought Beth, but it still made her feel absolutely dreadful. He had once said, "I'm so sorry...for everything." And she had once said, "You have my forgiveness always. Always." That should – there's that word again...SHOULD...have been the end of it, so why did it feel so awful now? What was left to do? "What am I missing?" she thought. "Why is this not sitting right? There is something left to do. What is it?" He will certainly go on punishing himself, probably for evermore, unless someone can make him see. Ha! Granny! 'There are none so blind as those who will not see.' OK, so he has to see. He doesn't know his own story...give him the draft of the book to read? Maybe. Then just pray he does see. Until then, Beth decided, she was no longer going to be picked up and discarded every time James felt like it. Perhaps he would be in a pickle when he made contact, maybe he would want a conversation, and maybe he did just want to see her. Even so, the thought that they had met in this lifetime to be there for each other filtered through. His job was to give the memories, hers to write it all down and show him. The children were back...the maid's son in the form of Daniel – such a strong young man in character and action; the wench's son in the form of Charlotte – a young lady full of giving. They were both such beautiful souls, kind, giving, strong, and would stand up for others. They wouldn't let others suffer. As yet, they didn't know why. She didn't know what to do about James being in her heart but it seemed clear that they had been brought together to help each other. James to give her that final piece of jigsaw and Beth, through her understanding and writing, to give him the means to understand his life. And she had to forgive. That was the killer realisation...she had to forgive. If he could face and give her all his weaknesses, less than chivalrous behaviour and his inability to deal with things the right way – by giving her the ammunition to 'go public' so to speak – then could she muster up the courage to forgive him? No, that wasn't right either because she had already given him her forgiveness for all time when she said, "You have my forgiveness, always." Right now she didn't feel like honouring that statement. Forgive Hazel? Never! Not this year, not next year...not in a million years! Forgive that one and she would laugh all the way into eternity enjoying the fact that she could carry on destroying Beth's soul forever and get away with it. Not a charitable thought and not the right way to look at things as a spiritualist. Today she was just going to be Beth and remembered her father saying, "Charity begins at home, maid. When you are in a good enough place to help others then that is the time to do it." Well, she wasn't in a good enough place yet and that felt a long way off. Meanwhile she had to get a grip, get a life...and live it. Preferably not in the shadow of someone else. So that is what she would do.

Beth switched on her phone and strode out the miles and headed for home – she had been gone five hours. The rest of the day was sort of already mapped out now: Kettle on, sandwich, biscuit, chocolate, iPad. Click on Essay and carry on with the book.

Buzz buzz. I'm so sorry. I didn't know what to say to you – still don't. Sorry isn't enough by a long chalk. I really need to speak with you, to talk properly to you. God, I've really let you down and hurt you haven't I? Please may I talk to you? Beth, please. J

Her heart missed a beat when she saw that message and six other similar ones. The spark was still there between them. It wasn't over yet. And Beth wondered how the book would end.

CHAPTER FOURTEEN

Mayrie put the pages down and said nothing. Neither did her gran. After a moment or two Amber put her hands over her granddaughter's hands and gazed lovingly into her eyes.

"Mayrie...what are you thinking?"

"Actually, gran, I'm thinking wow, this is a very real story...great grandma could certainly write a living tale, couldn't she? It is like the reader is standing in it and watching...the past is here and I, as the reader, am living it," answered Mayrie. "Why? What are you thinking?"

Amber took a breath as if measuring up what to say next.

"I'm thinking it is time I contacted a couple of old friends of mine and maybe you could take me to visit them."

"Who gran? Do I know them? Where do they live?"

"No, darling, I don't think you do know them...James Lindley and Megan Harvey...and luckily they both live in the same area – Oxford – so not far enough away to make a trip difficult. We could probably benefit from staying away overnight but I'm up for it, are you?" asked gran with the beginnings of a twinkle in her eyes.

"You already know the answer to that, gran," said Mayrie. "Of course I am. Hurry up and make the arrangements...I can't wait to find out what this is all about because you aren't going to tell me, are you?"

"No, darling, I'm not. This is something we can do together," replied Amber. "But I think it is time I went to bed now. If I am to meet this young man tomorrow I need to look my best. Goodnight darling."

"Goodnight gran. Sleep well."

Mayrie wasn't ready for sleep so began to re-read *Consider This* and it was 8am when she was woken by the sound of cups clinking in the kitchen, finding herself in the big old comfy chair and the manuscript still in her hand.

"Gran? Make me one, please," she groaned. "I could really do with a cup of tea."

"Done, darling, and breakfast is ready," came the soft reply. "And that thing has been flashing."

Mayrie checked her messages; one from work confirming her chat with them earlier in the week, and one from Anni saying that, if it was OK with her, she and Roshan would be along at 10am.

Anticipation was running high between Mayrie and Amber, neither able to disguise their excitement at the prospect of Roshan being able to get some information from all the technical wizardry of yesteryear and neither wanting to think about the possibility of it not happening. They both got themselves ready for their visitors, gran much more quietly than Mayrie, and the box of their hopes sat on the kitchen table, waiting to spill its secrets. The knock on the door finally came and Anni introduced the very tall, dark and handsome man standing beside her as her much older brother. He put on a well-practised expression that was supposed to cover the easy-going and loving relationship between him and his sister, which served no purpose at all because everyone could see through it straightaway.

"Not MUCH older...only two years, Anni."

To which she rejoined, "Ah, yes, but I am only 28 which makes you 30...a different decade...so, much older."

It was obvious those two shared a wonderful bond but it didn't stop there; Anni was kind, gentle and lovely to everyone and, as it turned out, so was her brother. Introductions over and tea and an array of biscuits and cake put out, it was time for the box to be opened. Roshan started to lift the flaps, not a breath to be heard, and all eyes fixed on his face. He took out each item slowly, examined it and put it on the table before taking the next and repeating the exercise, finally looking first at Amber and then at Mayrie and said...absolutely nothing. He grinned from ear to ear.

"Is it any good, Roshan?" asked Amber.

"Mrs. Jones, this is absolutely marvellous. You have no idea what potential fun you have just presented me with. Would you please let me take this away to work on? I won't even have to take it back to London because my time here has been extended to six months..."

Anni interjected, "And WHEN were you planning on telling me that? Is the memory going already, old man?"

"Sorry, An. By the way, my time here has been extended to six months – can I stay with you or shall I find somewhere else, Little One?"

"You most certainly will NOT find somewhere else! You will stay with us – as well you know, you idiot!" she laughed.

"Oh, that's good, because you know that case I told you not to touch and is still in your car? Well, it is full of stuff I might need for playing with Mrs. Jones's things...if it is all right with you, Mrs. Jones?"

"Please call me gran or Amber," said Amber. "I'm not one for standing on ceremony, my dear."

"Gran it is, then...so if it is all right with you, gran, I have something with me that might get that iPad working...shall we have a look now?" asked Roshan, with the hopeful look of a puppy on his face.

She looked at Mayrie as an invitation for her to answer that question, knowing all too well that she would say yes.

It wasn't long before Roshan could announce, "Gran, Mayrie, we are in business. Let's see what we have. Where would you like me to look first, photos and videos or documents?"

"Photos and videos, please," they answered together.

"Here we go then ladies. All you do is gently run a finger across the screen like this to get to the next picture...all yours," said Roshan, his eyes full of compassion for these two lovely women – one of whom was about to walk down memory lane and the other about to visit a time in history long before her birth.

Amber invited Anni and Roshan to gather round so that they could see the images as well. The quality of the pictures was not as good as nowadays, of course, but it was pretty good and Amber had no difficulty in recognising the people and places. There were several of Jack and Emily, and of her.

"When do you think these were taken, gran? You look very young!" asked Roshan, eager to know roughly what year had been brought to life for him to share.

"I would guess it was not too long before I went to university, which was 2014," answered Amber. "This is my dad and that is my gran – they both died in 2015 if I remember correctly. Oh my! This is a good one of Jack and Emily, Mayrie...handsome boy wasn't he? That is mum's friend, Frances, and that is a group of her church friends."

Mayrie noticed gran's lingering touch on the face of a man in the group but said nothing.

After a sigh Amber continued, "That one is Alison...she was a hoot; I don't know who the children are...probably something to do with her friends...if they had been looking at the camera I may have recognised them."

The next pictures were of scenery, which stirred Mayrie into excitement. "Gran! It's the weir...it IS the weir...look! She must have liked it there – oh! gran! The other day... Don't you think that is what it means – that she liked it there, I mean?"

Gran gave a silent nod seen only by Mayrie. "Can we see if there are any videos, please?" asked Amber, and Roshan showed them how to view them.

The first one showed a lady and a man sitting at a table talking. The voice of a man asked, "Peter? Tea or coffee? What about you, Debbie?"

And the voice of another man, obviously that of the person holding the iPad, saying, "That's tea all round then Max."

Mayrie could hold it in no longer. "Gran, what is your mum doing with three men?"

"No idea, darling. I was in Canada then...look at the calendar on the wall. Maybe we'll find out," she answered.

To see her great grandma moving and speaking was magical to Mayrie and she watched avidly, wishing it never to end. The one called Max came into the picture bearing mugs of tea but when Debbie moved declaring she was fetching biscuits both Peter and Max reacted like overprotective mothers. Debbie was in a wheelchair.

"I knew she'd had an accident and broken her legs," said Amber. "But never got any real details about it...she seemed to want to forget it as quickly as possible. Reasonable, I suppose. Peter and Max I remember were friends of hers but as to who is behind the camera is a bit of a mystery at the moment as the voices aren't too clear to me, but it is clearly a friend. Let's have a look at the next one, shall we?" she quickly asked in the hope that no-one had spotted her little fib.

The next video was of Debbie on crutches, walking very badly and again with Peter and Max in attendance and the unknown cameraman. A third video showed Debbie having progressed from using crutches to walking with sticks, but this time it seemed to be some kind of occasion rather than just a gathering of friends. There was Debbie, and Peter and Max, another man, a uniformed young woman and an older man in an even more impressive uniform. Amber's eyes keened up and she looked intently at the group. Max turned to Peter and said something, squeezing his hand and holding on to it. The words hadn't been picked up on the recording but Amber smiled and nodded to herself as she lip-read, "I am so proud of you."

The two uniformed people stood and the man delivered a short speech: "Ladies and Gentlemen, we are here today because of the courage, determination and dedication of Debbie, Peter, Andrew, Max and my officer, Detective Sergeant McGoldrick and, of course, all of the wonderful doctors and nurses. All I am going to say today is that I totally agree with everything that Rachael is about to say and so, without more delay, I hand you over to DS Rachael McGoldrick."

Then it was the turn of the uniformed lady who said: "Debbie Bayfield, you are an extraordinary woman. I have come to know you very well and am pleased to now be counted amongst your friends. Had it not been for the actions of Peter there would have been a very different outcome indeed. It was an honour to have been assigned the job of protecting you when necessary and it is no understatement when I say you have been an inspiration to more people than you could possibly realise. The hospital staff, the police officers, these guys here...you have inspired us all. Peter, thank you for keeping Debbie alive at the beginning of all this and, Max, thank you for joining Peter in continuing to care for Debbie. Andrew, thank you for the difficult path you trod, although I believe you actually didn't find it difficult at all when you finally admitted something to yourself. The dedication and love you have all given has been an important factor in Debbie's recovery. Debbie, I have been given special permission to give you this. It never was part of the formal proceedings and so need not remain in the possession of the Police Force; it would only be destroyed. However, because you have touched all our hearts with your bravery and determination, not to mention humility, I have the greatest pleasure in presenting this to...Andrew, who will give it to you shortly...won't you, Andrew? You know what this is don't you, Andrew? Man, is it ever time!"

Rachael's facial expressions flitted from serious, to genuine care, to mock exasperation.

Andrew's face showed embarrassment, Debbie looked confused, Peter and Max gave one another a hug and kiss, the two police officers smiled broadly and applause could be heard all around as Andrew was given something very small...something that looked suspiciously like one of the cassettes found in the boxes. Then the picture flashed to the faces of two grinning children and back again to Andrew. Roshan explained that the children would have been filming the event – an iPad had the facility to 'reverse film' as he put it.

"So that is Andrew, but exactly what was that all about?" thought Mayrie, deciding not to ask out loud. There was something about gran's expression, which told her that now was not the time.

"There are more videos," announced Roshan. "But I'm afraid this temporary enablement is precisely that – temporary – so we can't view any more right now. Sorry to disappoint you."

As he was being told that it was certainly no disappointment because they had plenty of other written stuff to go through, and that he had given them much more than he could ever imagine, Roshan turned over another piece of equipment, before saying, "I think I can do one more thing today. If I am right about this all I need do is put this...here – take that and put it...there – then stick this bit in...yes, here... OK, let's see what this magnificent thing can do. Gran, can you remember how this works?"

Much to Amber's surprise she did and she asked someone to pass her one of the things she called a CD.

"There's already one in there, gran. Here, let me quickly wipe it over, although everything is so clean I can't see any dust here at all. You have had this well wrapped," laughed Roshan. "There you go. Make it work its magic."

And with that Amber pressed a button and, after a little whirring, lovely piano music filled the room. Everyone fell silent, listening to the ease of the notes and appreciating the exceptional calmness it brought.

Barely audible, Mayrie's words bounced around the room like thunder, "I've heard this before – recently."

Amber asked, equally quietly, "When, darling?"

She was not completely surprised when Mayrie said, "Monday, on my way to you. At the weir."

Anni was watching both of them, taking in every look on their faces with barely disguised emotion. She knew this was something big and had an inkling of what it was, knowing that it could be almost too much for either or both of them. No, she thought to herself. Gran would be all right; her face carried the graceful smile of complete calm and understanding.

Amber stopped the music, lifted the lid and handed the CD to Mayrie who read the label: 'Secret Cascades of the Soul,' written and played by Andrew Lindley.

Gran gazed into her granddaughter's eyes and held that contact as she explained that Andrew was the Andrew they had just seen in the videos and that her mother, Debbie, had always declared it her favourite piece of music.

Anni thought it was time to speak up and suggested that perhaps it was time she and her brother left them to mull over all they had seen and heard, especially as gran was probably a bit tired and would appreciate a rest, something which Amber quickly put to one side and countered with her own idea of them all going out to lunch together. She won, of course, and when they came home she and Mayrie decided to look through the journals or the other manuscript together...after gran had made arrangements with James and Megan to meet. She told James that they had found something interesting in her mum's possessions and would very much like to show it to them both and talk about it. Gran had been enigmatic in her wording but Mayrie had the distinct impression that James had a good understanding of what was happening. On Monday she and gran would be heading for Oxford and staying the night with James but for now it was story time and Mayrie began sifting through her great-grandmother's journals, which had been so lovingly stored for so many years.

"Right, then, gran...here we go," Mayrie said with anticipation, and began putting them in chronological order, which took far longer than she expected.

Amber, unobserved, picked up the smaller manuscript with one tantalising word scribbled across the top... 'Unfinished' ...and began to read.

After a while Mayrie heard a subtle change in Amber's breathing and noticed she was reading. She couldn't see what her gran was reading but she could see that she was struggling with something just as she did after reading the two poems and, although her mind was full of questions, she chose wisely which ones she asked.

Sunday seemed to last forever which was just as well because it gave them both time to gather together what they needed to take to Oxford. Even better, it had given Roshan time to get the thing gran had called the cassette player working and, because of the tape he had heard when checking his workmanship, he decided gran probably should have it without delay. Mayrie wasn't there when he delivered it to gran and, knowing the explosive nature of it, Roshan asked if he could sit with her whilst she listened to it as he felt she really should have someone with her when she did. He pressed the button and they listened in stunned silence:

"It is 15:05 on Monday, 16 October 2017. Present in the room are Andrew Lindley and Detective Sergeant Rachael McGoldrick."

"Protect Debbie? What do you mean protect her? Why?"

"We protect anyone who we suspect is the victim of attempted murder – this is not a formal interview..."

"Murder? You think someone ran her down on purpose? But why?"

"This is merely to record what is said between us. You are not under suspicion...we know you were working when Debbie was knocked over and left for dead."

"Then what do you want with me, Rachael? Uh...am I allowed to call you Rachael? Should I call you something else if this is police business? Why did she react like that when all I wanted to do was kiss her goodbye? I don't understand."

"Rachael is fine, Andrew. I have a photograph to show you...do you recognise this at all?"

"What has this got to do with Debbie's accident?"

"It was found in Debbie's hand when the ambulance crew were tending to her. We think she grabbed it when whoever ran her down probably also tried to strangle her."

"STRANGLE? Strangle? No! Not Debbie! Who would want to kill her? No...no...can't be. Rachael, whoever did this, you get them and you throw the key away. Do you hear me? Throw the key away!

I see you, Debbie. I know who you are. I'm not leaving you again."

Gran was grateful to Roshan for staying with her. It was a part of her mother's life which she had never known and it came as quite a shock and yet not really a surprise in the wake of what was unravelling in her mind. She would take this and play it to James and Megan.

CHAPTER FIFTEEN

It surprised Mayrie to see the affection between James, Megan and her gran. Gran had never talked of them so to witness affection rather than friendship was, in Mayrie's eyes, quite strange. Her stomach did a flip, her heart raced a little and there was something familiar about this and yet nothing was familiar at all. James and Megan, who, it turned out, were brother and sister, were both quite a few years younger than gran and she knew she had never met them before. The surprise that Mayrie was anticipating did not let her down. Amber produced the manuscripts and invited James and Megan to read them. Megan picked up the larger one, read the title, and gave James a knowing look; he remained silent but returned the look. Something was going on here, thought Mayrie as she glanced at gran who had also taken in the silent conversation between the other two. She put it down and picked up the smaller one and this time the fire of interest was evident in the pair of them. Megan prepared to read so that James could hear and, periodically, little looks passed between the two and there were almost indiscernible nods of their heads. Mayrie fought to still her tongue, again, so desperately she wanted to ask questions but she would have to wait. She could hear uncertain anticipation in Megan's voice as she began.

UNFINISHED

Beth had to take her time. She had to sort things out in her mind and there was only one place where she might stand a chance of doing that. Over the years she had found solace, peace, fortitude and a safe haven at the weir. It was a place where she could ask any question without feeling embarrassment. Here she could cry, scream, shout or reveal her innermost secrets. It felt wonderful to share such things where they would be listened to and carried away with no questions asked, no reprisals, no accusations.

This was a particularly difficult time and she had a monumental problem. A difficult task lay ahead. Her spiritual beliefs had served her well and she had found a couple of clairvoyants whose abilities were without doubt first class and undisputed, certainly where Beth was concerned. They tuned in to her completely and she knew she could trust what they said to her. If they didn't know or weren't sure, they would say so. One of them did tarot cards and the other was clearly an exceptionally gifted clairvoyant. It wasn't a belief which sat well with everyone, just as any religion or even atheism is not for everyone. Of course, there was much more to spiritualism than clairvoyance which is something many people didn't want to recognise and so they never ventured into it. Beth had learned to balance the belief with the 'showmanship' of clairvoyance. What was playing on her mind now was a new clairvoyant who had recently given her a message...had given her much more than a message. She was going to have to go through it all again down at the weir. If clarity was to be had maybe the weir would offer it.

Beth had been really upset when James had taken up with Hazel and she tried really hard to step away, but it seemed an impossible task. As far as James knew she had succeeded and she would never tell him how her heart was still holding him. They agreed to remain friends and James continued to greet her and say goodbye with a hug but it soon became apparent that he also seemed to be struggling with letting Beth go. He confided in Beth, he would smooth her hair without thinking about it, or put his arm around her waist and pull her close for a hug. Sometimes when they were chatting he would stop mid-sentence, his eyes would take on a deep, even sad, look and he would tell her she was beautiful and that he missed her. The hugs became embraces that lasted a long time and would turn into slow dances, and they would find themselves exploring each other's bodies and, yet, he would still return to Hazel.

James always tried to stop himself and the situation as soon as he realised where it was heading... 'his weakness'...

as he put it. Beth had never instigated anything between them, except in the very beginning when they had shared their very first kiss and James had said, "It was only a moment," and she had replied, "pity." She could not work out why she had said that – it was so out of character – and right there and then she resolved never to take the lead in anything of a romantic nature. If it was to happen then it would do so without her help; and so it had always been. James always made the moves, Beth just didn't stop them. This had gone on for months, leaving Beth with an inner conflict like she had never known before. He missed her; he needed her – yet he went back to Hazel. He was clearly trying to make it work with Hazel. If anything was meant to happen between James and Beth, if they were meant to be together, it would do so without Beth interfering. She would never put herself in the position of being accused of taking James away from Hazel, or any other woman. Beth and he certainly had an affinity with each other. There was something extraordinarily strong that pulled them together even though they tried to keep apart. Beth did not want it to become a problem.

Now Beth had something else to think about. She met a clairvoyant when she had taken herself off for a short break. She hadn't gone far, just up to Southampton to be near Charlotte, who was having a few struggles of her own at the time. Beth quietly assessed the clairvoyant, Sue, before deciding she had enough faith in her to make an appointment but, when the time came and she heard what Sue had to say, it wasn't at all what she was expecting. It left her reeling and upset, yet she knew it was completely right and that she had a fight on her hands. In fact, she faced nothing short of a spiritual Armageddon. She shouldn't have been surprised, given the information she entrusted to Sue after the session. That was what had driven her to seeking out someone like Sue; someone who didn't know her or her situation, or anyone else involved in it. What Sue told her made perfect sense, but to give James up totally, to cut him out of her life completely, to never have contact with him again...that was awful, too awful to contemplate. Beth wanted to cry.

Sue had told her that there were people who didn't like her, who had attached hooks to her and were psychically attacking her. She picked up on a woman and was instantly and particularly worried by her and what she may do. Her face was full of concern and her voice was alarmingly sincere. "She works with dark forces, she has hooks into you, she hates you, and there is someone else in it with her...they are working together on it. Maybe the other one isn't quite aware of what is happening, but she is using him to get to you so that she can take your energy. She is getting your energy through emotion with the other person, a man...you have to cut him out of your life completely. If you have contact with him you will give him your energy and emotion and he will carry it...she will then take it from him. She feeds off of you via him. You have to stop it happening. They will suck you dry. But he also has to tell her to stop...he has to get away from her. They are chasing you through the centuries for some kind of wrong they think has been done."

Beth then told Sue about the three lives she knew about and how, in each of them, the scene had been the same. Hazel had been the controller, James had been the controlled and Beth had been the victim. The perceived wrong was, as far as Beth could see, that James had in each case favoured her over Hazel and Hazel had always made it her mission to take him away, or someone away, from Beth. And it was happening all over again in this life.

She also told Sue how she had, inexplicably, one day shaken herself and said with unexpected force, "And you can get off my back as well. Go on, run away." She had seen a hairy black thing, triangular in shape, with long black bony talon-like fingers and toes scuttle away squealing louder, and nastier, than a stuck pig.

"It was her, Sue, I know it was and I'm terrified she'll hurtle back with a tenfold force," admitted Beth. Sue also told Beth that not only was this woman working with the dark side but there was such evil, the thought of which frightened Beth intensely. The thought that she was up against pure evil and that it was her job to obliterate it from her life and James's life was too much to contemplate; she might as well give up right then because she had no idea of how to do it. Sue then said that the woman was not as strong as she thought she was; Beth was stronger, much stronger. The woman was becoming angry because she couldn't deal with the light that shone from Beth, or the goodness that was within her, or the love that she sent out and suggested that she encase her adversary in a bubble of light – she wouldn't like it – and do it with love. It would weaken her even more, but Beth had to be extremely careful, ground herself and lay down heavy protection; centre, ground and protect was the instruction. Instinctively she knew that to do so for just herself was far from enough so she included every friend, every family member, pets and their respective houses inside and out, including all chimney flues and pipes leading into the houses. She did their vehicles; she did absolutely everything she could think of and a bit more. And she did the same for James. She had a very bad feeling about all of this.

CHAPTER SIXTEEN

As usual, Beth could hear the water tumbling over the weir before she got there and the sound always excited her, made her sparkle inside as she marvelled at the sight that would greet her. As she paced round the bend in the lane she could see the mound of grass in the middle of the river. Whenever there had been rain it would become submerged but not today. There had been no rain for a week. She stepped into the little space by the fence, already aware of something different. Please, please, please, please, please, please... The water was speaking as it cascaded over the stones, its message sounding rather urgent even though the flow of water was no faster than usual. Then she saw it. A huge dome of foam had amassed at the foot of the weir and was just sitting at the side, precisely where she stood to watch. It must have been 3ft in diameter and proportionately domed. Never before had she seen foam like that...only the bubbles which the crashing water always created and which had always been carried away with the water's journey down the river.

So softly, she whispered, "Spirit, what does this mean, what are you trying to tell me?" and that is when the half-ball of foam began to spin.

It seemed a very long time before she began the walk home none the wiser as to its meaning, but she pondered on it for the rest of the day. When she met Alison and Anne for coffee she described it to them but neither could put any significance to it. That evening, having changed into her fluffy jammies, Beth lit a bevy of tea lights, sat quietly in her favourite armchair, closed her eyes and tried to meditate. Nothing. She opened her eyes and stared at the flames of the little candles throwing out such a beautiful, gentle light. Suddenly the knowledge was there: Water is energy, energy is emotion, and therefore, foam is created out of emotion. It was half a ball so the 'please' meant 'please give me the other half of the ball...my energy needs your energy to make me whole'.

Beth's mind asked, "But what do I make of that? What do I do with it?" The answer was immediate, becoming knowledge almost before the question was completely asked. Ignore it. Foam is not solid, this is not a solid request or plea. It is a trick. It was spinning to mesmerise you but was also representative of the urgency for your energy that the requester was feeling.

Beth thought about Sue's words. "She uses him to get to you...she feeds off you via him. You must not give her your energy and that is why you must sever all connection with this man."

Without having made a conscious decision Beth went to find the reading Naomi had given her, made a cup of tea and then sat down to read it and consider Sue's warning. "If I withdraw, she still takes from him. He is sucked dry. Both Alison and Valerie think she will wreck his life, spit him out and then say, 'There you are, you can have him now," Beth thought, and then she read the brief notes she had made of Naomi's reading.

Saw things for 7 months ahead, which also takes us to May. She saw a reunion or someone coming into my life; more focus; at some time getting energies – which are currently fragmented – back. She saw the bereavement card, which could mean emotional detachment as well as physical detachment. An uphill struggle with emotions and betrayal, past life stuff. Huge, massive sorrow and resentment. Light at end of tunnel but must keep on with sadness yet. Sorrow cannot be ignored. Then came the energies back...she saw 1 male 1 female, me + 1; the "two of us" walking parallel lines and we have to watch each other doing it. Wanting to talk of happiness for both of us. If it brings us together eventually, so be it. A strange journey. Unusual circumstances. The cards say it is strange. It all pivots on him and his ability to grow some balls...get a grip of the true situation. The "problem" was recognised by cards. He needs to believe in himself and his work; needs to focus and not be got at by "the problem." I am treading a fine line. Keys of opportunity – find the right door. Doors to unlock. Trust my helpers. A difficult situation...be honest with self but don't put self in wrong place. Everything is minute – I must go ahead and let him see I can get on without him. Can't be in his world because he won't allow it but he wants it...got me on a string. He needs to get away from everything until cleared head. Too much emotion, screwing him and me up. Two worlds running parallel. I know there is a pot of gold there – he's looking for it. Cards showed success after struggles. Will feel "at last" at least 7 months down the line. Improvement. See end results, reassurance. After the bereavement card she saw child custody battles, family get-together, power again; control business. I think relates to James as no children in my family. After that came the hangman. I have to tread water for 12 months and the end of that heralds new beginnings, as shown by the next card of success after struggles. After this came a person acting like a petulant child, stroppy, always one step ahead, hyperactive. H? Then I get a happy event, a distraction. Things will work out but N couldn't see in what way. The next card suggested Daniel was bringing the happy surprises. Could be a pregnancy.

Then Beth started to listen to the CD of Naomi's reading and her voice began:

(Obviously I know a lot about your circumstances because I've known you a very long time, but these are the cards you have chosen and I shall relate to you exactly what they represent...so...here we go with the first card...

Listen. Go with gut feelings. New beginnings. Still in process...being sorted. Follow feelings and get it going in right direction. Timing – not yet there. Keep going with tenacity and perseverance. Follow Spirit and intuition. Don't pre-empt. Trust feelings. Will get result but it will come about in a different way. Look to past to propel forward...learn from past to see where to go now. Use knowledge and experience as a reference. Got stamina and inner wisdom...dig deep and discover it...use it...You've hidden it rather well.

Your Spirit Guide has brought in the King of Swords as your Guide also. I first thought this card was J but this time I think it really represents your dad. He is helping a lot and is increasing your spiritual intuitiveness. Has a very strong personality, very black and white. He wants you to know he's guiding and guarding you through the hullabaloo, that's the word he is using; haha, you are nodding so is that one of his words? He has obviously given me that one as proof to you that it is him, and he is saying it is the hullabaloo of lots of emotions. All options are there – money, love, joy, etc, emotions, working towards, flying high. You must connect with Dad and Guide and concentrate your thoughts on them – it will take time but you mustn't give up. Here I see J like a lost sheep, floundering, lost his focus, wandering in the desert. Someone is trying to make him go where he doesn't want to go. He's got to grow some – I can't say that! Well, I'm being told to say it so I will – he's got to grow some balls. He'd appreciate opinions but not act on them; he has to change that.

Next is Queen of Swords which represents two people we know. One is H, the other is mum. In this case I feel it is your mum although it is parallel situations!! It is a darker haired lady playing up. J is like a lamb to the slaughter...the penny should have dropped by now...that is what they are saying about growing some, um.. things. This is a card showing a young person, or one who acts in a young way, ... music is important to them – either playing or learning, happy, sociable, bubble of love, intuitive. Think this is J but could also be you. This darker haired lady manipulates this child...he's almost taken her on as a mother. She controls him

– he likes the motherly ordering. She's treating him as a child. This is also you and your mother. She squashed your dreams. They are saying this is a whole big pot of emotions. A real toughie...all these emotions brought you to this...it's ongoing.

The next cards are really thumping home the message of lessons – oh! this is unusual – of past lives! – of sorrow, sad, deep feelings, resentment, struggle, betrayal. See an uphill struggle for you with emotions, betrayal of every life they are saying. Spirit is telling me to talk of past lives and here it is again...an ongoing lesson. There is light at the end of the tunnel but have to keep on with the sadness yet, it is a massive, huge, sack of sorrow and it can't be ignored. This is not a very nice message for me to deliver...are you OK for me to continue? Yes? Good. If it was anyone but you sitting there I would struggle a bit to disguise the brutality of it. However, Dad is acknowledging the fact he's supporting you, could see what was going on but incapable of doing anything and regrets not doing or saying more. He is aware of gradual knock-on effect all the time. I feel you two have been in a life or lives before. Huge unity between dad and you. I see an eternal triangle of dad, J and you... (I don't quite understand that one, Naomi,..him, me and mum definitely, but I haven't come across dad in any of the lives I can put to me and J). It's a power thing, Beth. Interesting. (Ah, Naomi... a thought just came to me...maybe it is now a power thing...dad has entered the equation and that is why it is now a triangle...me and dad, and J.)

Next cards...good to see this next one. This brings in happy times and relationship in the future or you will be happy in current one. Definitely happiness coming in. Getting energies back into normality. Fragmented energies at the moment. This shows a male and a female...you + a male. He's got to do his bit, and you yours. You are walking parallel lines – must watch each other. Wanting to talk of happiness for both of you. If it brings you together eventually, so be it. It has been a strange journey so far. Unusual circumstances. Even the cards are saying so. It all pivots on him and his ability to grow some balls – get a grip. The Queen of Swords is his problem regarding his work, he needs to believe in himself, needs to focus, not be "got at" by this woman. The Taurean card represents April/May. I see father/grandfather link. (Grandad's birthday 8 May, dad was buried on 8 May, and Michael's birthday 8 May – will that do, Naomi?). It certainly will, Beth. Grandad has joined forces with dad; a joint drive – let's get on. Keep driving forward – be you – don't put things on hold – don't pre-empt or hold back. Take the middle line, tiptoe along but you can't keep going forward without saying anything. You're treading a fine line. Eventually will have to do something or get disillusioned, etc. I see keys of opportunity. Doors to unlock. Find the right key for the right door. Is it this one or that one? Again stay in the middle but the decision is yours alone. Trust your helpers. The way to go is the way you feel you can cope with life in that direction. Difficult – must be honest with yourself but not put yourself in wrong place. Gosh, this is minute! It could signify a possible house move, hence the key. One thing at a time. Could be – not yet – another family member moving out. Not easy cards, are they?

Here's the bereavement card. Down the line, when mum goes, stuff changes. Lots hanging in the air. In a nutshell the message is that 10 months' time will see disruption, sadness, sorting out, letting go of emotions, sorting, sifting, looking ahead. Divert your attention to a new subject. Get rid of the old. Complex situation – many things. Decide where you want to go and don't stop yourself just because others not ready to step up. As they see you going on well it will give them a jolt. Spirit is asking me to pass this on...try to appear not that bothered...put the boot on the other foot.

Next cards are showing...reunion or getting together, or a family thing. Waiting for things to happen...interesting... treading water...in suspension...meanwhile get on with things. Sibling rivalry is shown here and here again is sorting out. This speaks of a 12-month period and this is encouraging you to take control. (My interpretation is that that would all seem to indicate mum passing over, Naomi. That's OK, I can deal with that).

So, here we have siblings, custody battles over children, family get together. Power again...control business. (There are no children, minors, in my family, Naomi. Could that mean something else?) Your worlds – J and you – parallel again. Strange that parallels being repeated for you. So much there. Hangman – tread water for 12 months – the end of that heralds new beginnings. This is the pregnancy card – put that out of equation it seems to say...the meaning here is new beginnings.

The next cards are comforting...success after struggles. Will feel "at last!" at least 7 months down the line. Improvement. Seeing end results. Reassurance.

But then we have an adult acting as a child. Hyperactive. Always a step ahead. Bit stroppy. Petulant behaviour. Unfortunate. I feel it could possibly be H.

It is all here again...a repeated message...Pondering, analysing, sadness, deep questions of what/if/etc. Happy event coming in – a distraction. Things will work out but just how, I can't see. Think next card is Daniel – hard working, reliable, younger man and it is all happening for him. Providing. Things will happen around him in a good way. Happy surprises. 7 months' time brings changes. Money, choices, decisions.

This card represents a determined lady – could be Charlotte. Someone going forward. Resolute and loyal to cause. Economics. Watch Charlotte and a new relationship.

Now this card is for a man over 40. Conscientious, hard working...J? Yes? Anyone else come to mind Beth? They don't? Oh, OK. He is turning this way and that way – how to do it? Financial connotations, practicalities and probably more concerned than he is letting on. Thinking of his children's futures.

I can't believe this...it is here again...there is a new relationship for you...maybe also for Charlotte. Two worlds running parallel, you know there's a pot of gold there, and he is looking for it. You must go ahead and let him see you can get on without him. You can't be in his world because he won't allow it but he wants it...got you on a string. He needs to get away from everything until he has cleared his head. There is too much emotion and it is screwing him up, and you.

The recording ended.

She put the pages down, closed her eyes and rubbed them hard, stopped, inhaled and held her breath briefly before exhaling fast and loud. She didn't breathe in again for a while. "I have to do as Sue says...but I can't...the thought hurts too much. Oh, dear God, give me the strength I need...PLEASE," she silently prayed, as a couple of tears rolled from her eyes. She swallowed hard and repeatedly thought, "I have to do this, I have to do this...she will not feed off of me...I refuse point blank to allow her to do that." And then, unannounced, clarity leapt in bringing with it the message, "It is time to think of me; there has been too much hurt – it stops here and now. I will not contact James again; I will not see him again. They will not hurt me again. I am free; I do not have to think about it any more. No more wondering, no more hoping, no more agonising, no more being picked up and put down. No more being taken for the fool I have allowed. I am taking charge of my life here and now. Goodbye James, goodbye Hazel. Sink or swim...I don't care...whichever it is, it will be without me." She picked up her mobile and deleted all but one message from James and then she deleted his number. Her eyes closed, she put her free hand to her forehead and, without being noticed, the phone slipped from the other hand on to the floor. She sat, still and quiet, with not a single thought registering, for a long while.

When she finally opened her eyes Beth felt...relieved! "What a surprise," she thought. "I feel relieved." What a remarkable journey that day had been; even more remarkable was the past two hours, to have moved from not being able to let him go to having let him go and feeling so relieved and free. This deserved a well-earned present to herself and that present was to be another cup of tea and a whole packet of chocolate digestives. She knew she wouldn't eat them all and, in fact, probably would have no more than five at the very most, but it was fun to think she could, and would, eat the whole lot if she wanted to. She deserved it.

CHAPTER SEVENTEEN

TWELVE MONTHS LATER

It had been a tough 18 months for Beth. Michael had died in April and her mother had died in June, leaving Beth with the job of sorting out everything – her house, finances, executing the will, etc., etc. Well, Naomi's words had come true...buckets full of sadness, sorting, sifting, new beginnings. The biggest surprise of all was Daniel and Emily announcing that Daniel had been offered a promotion. What welcome news after the events of the year so far.

She and James had not been in contact – James had tried but Beth ignored his attempts. He had chosen Hazel and that was that. Beth had seen him around and heard various bits and pieces about him, none of which she actively sought out. It did, however, get back to her that he had been watching her life unfold too. So, perhaps things weren't quite so rosy in his garden after all. "Oh dear, what a shame!" she thought rather sarcastically, and then berated herself for having done so as it was against all her beliefs to relish in others' misfortunes. Nothing ever warranted that but the hurt ran deep and just thinking about it made her attentions turn to Charlotte who had taken the deaths of her gran and father quite badly. She was feeling quite desperate for the summer holidays and, quite honestly, Beth couldn't wait either. To have Charlotte home again to look after was a lovely thought. At that precise moment Beth needed to feel wanted but before anything else she wanted to come to grips with the way she had been thinking. To realise she was having less than decent humanitarian thoughts about 'certain people' was a wake up call; this was not who she wanted to be...everyone has their own life and that is precisely what it is...their own life. Even so, she could see that maybe a little divine intervention could be called for and she sent out a prayer for James.

"Sacred Spirit, Angels of Light, Guides and Guardians, please help James in all of his endeavours and do not let him fall victim to any untoward malice or bad feeling, and please keep him safe from her...from Hazel's influence. She is no good for him, and it truly pains me to say that but he does need your protection from her. I do love him in a way I can't really explain except to say that in many, if not all, ways we seem to be the two sides of the same thing. Isn't it funny how love takes so many different forms yet each is of the same depth and strength? No wonder it is so difficult to know if we love someone enough to marry them. How do we know if it is friend-love, empathy-love, marriage-love or even temporary love? What is the deciding factor? So, getting back to the point, please help James with everything he has to do, and give him the strongest protection you can. Holly needs him. Please put my love with yours and direct it his way. He doesn't have to know I'm sending it. Oh, and please direct it to Daniel, Emily and Charlotte. They all seem to be OK with everything but lots of love is never too much. Thank you for listening, Spirit." Shortly after that Beth had an odd, random thought; 'the heart and soul of the matter,' and then gave a brief wry laugh at the significance of that phrase.

It was in the middle of the holidays when the biggest surprise arrived.

Buzz buzz. Please, can we meet?

Write message: Um...who is this? You have not come up as a recognised number. Press send.

Buzz buzz: Please, Beth. I know I don't deserve it...but please. James

Write message: Oh! I don't know. Give me one good reason why I should even consider it. B. Press send.

Buzz buzz: Because I hurt you beyond redemption.

Buzz buzz: Because I owe you more than an apology but even if I start now and don't stop until I die it will never be enough. J

Write message: I don't think it would be a good idea, James. You will only hurt me all over again and I am not willing to put myself through it again. Once in a lifetime was bad enough – I will not allow it twice. Press send.

Buzz buzz: Beth I am so very, very sorry. I understand. J

Write message: No – you don't. You never saw who I was. Send message.

Buzz buzz: I saw a lovely woman with a beautiful, kind nature who understood me and made me feel wonderful but whose feelings I trampled and ignored. Is that what you mean? Please tell me...how can I apologise properly? J.

Write message: Where are you? Press send.

Buzz buzz: At home.

Write message: I shall be at the garden centre for another 20mins then I'm leaving to pick Charlotte up at the station. Press send.

Buzz buzz: OK. I'm on my way. Please don't leave, Beth. J.

She knew James would be there within ten minutes so she ordered a coffee for him and sat back to sip her tea until he arrived. Had she made the right decision? Well, she would soon find out. He must have driven like the wind because he was there in well under ten minutes...Beth didn't think it was possible, but he'd done it and James arrived at her table with apprehension written all over his face. Her heart skipped a beat which she wasn't expecting and immediately thought she had made the biggest mistake ever in letting him meet her, and then he spoke with a voice clearly struggling to cope with all the emotion welling up inside. "Beth, I...I...um...uh..." he faltered, resting his elbows on the table and burying his head heavily in his hands, and that is how he remained as he let out a deep breath and said, "Beth, I don't know what to say. I had it all planned out...have had it all planned out for a long time...and now I don't know what to say. Sorry, Beth, I'm so, so, sorry for hurting you and treating you so badly. It's not enough, but I don't know what else to say. I'm totally lost and I don't know what to do to make it right. Well, I can't make it right because it has happened and it was so wrong. What can I do Beth? Please forgive me, if you can, or even just a little bit of forgiveness would be a big thing. You are so special to me."

Beth said nothing for an eternal minute then raised her eyes from her teacup to see James still holding his head and in a gentle, yet commanding, voice said, "Look up James, look at me." Very slowly his eyes met hers. "Look into my eyes, James, really look and see my soul. Before you can do anything you have to recognise me."

Her earlier words played through his head 'once in a lifetime was bad enough' and he said, "Previous life...why didn't I see it before?" And answered himself by adding, "For some reason I didn't want to."

They sat without speaking for the next five minutes whilst James tried to absorb Beth's soul and she saw that he had seen...seen something he wished he had not.

Beth put her hand on his arm and said, "I'm sorry, I have to go now but I can tell by your face that...well, you have seen something. When you get home there are other souls to search as well – yours is one of them. I wish you courage."

They said their goodbyes and James just had time to give her hand a gentle squeeze before she walked away without looking back. He slumped in his chair, screwed up his eyes and asked, "What HAVE I done? Oh, Lord! What HAVE I done? Help me, please." He had never felt more sincere in his life than at that moment.

CHAPTER EIGHTEEN

The publisher was expecting Beth's latest novel on Monday so the next few days saw her making final preparations for its submission and, as usual, she decided to make three copies – one for submission, one to keep and an extra one for the simple reason of 'just in case.' This time, though, she was surprised to find that, actually, she had mistakenly made four copies and that cemented the half-thought that had been in her mind whilst writing it to give a copy to someone else prior to publishing. Perhaps it hadn't been a mistake after all, maybe it was something she was meant to do all along, but a letter explaining it seemed a better idea. The manuscript addressed to her publisher was packaged up and put ready for the courier to collect later that morning and then she would be meeting Anne at the pub for lunch. This is something they did on rare occasions but as Anne was going away for a couple of months they decided to have a special lunch and share all their news. Beth had quite a bit to tell. With the publisher's copy securely wrapped she then concentrated on writing the letter of explanation, a letter that could never be small, or easy to write. Sentences hesitatingly formed on the pages as she freed her caged thoughts, the hands of the clock gliding over the numbers as hour followed hour. It was a long time before Beth gathered the bundle of paper, satisfied with the content, and sealed it in a very large envelope.

Wednesday wasn't an overly warm day but the sun shone and cast its light wide. A pleasant day is what her dad would have called it. She was thinking a lot about him today and she smiled to herself as she remembered his phrases and stories, his voice so clear in her head.

"I miss you, dad," she said out loud. "Wish I could see you again."

"Take care, maid," she heard him say in that familiar mellow voice full of love and concern for his daughter.

"OK," she replied. "I hear you. Take care, yourself."

Courier gone, money in one pocket, mobile phone in another and clutching the letter, Beth set off to meet Anne at the pub. They spent a couple of hours laughing and catching up, Anne telling tales of her grandchildren and Beth informing her about Daniel and Emily and their new life in Canada. Daniel's company had offered him the opportunity to work in their Canadian branch for a few years and, although Beth and Charlotte would miss them terribly, they were both very pleased for their fortune and encouraged them to accept without a second thought. It was a new phase in all their lives – new and very different. Who could know what it might bring in the long term? It was exciting.

Feeling very full and very heavy, and having said goodbye to Anne, Beth started off on the long walk she had promised herself; it was what she always did when she had finished a book. Her bones, muscles and head needed detangling, as she put it, and the circular walk to the next two villages and back would take her on a 10-mile route. That would do nicely. The delivered bulging envelope landed with a thud behind the door, making Beth jump and then to immediately argue with herself as to whether she felt relieved or full of regret. Was it a wise thing to have done? How would James react? She didn't know she had been seen.

James lived in one of the older houses on the edge of the village so it wasn't far before she could turn right, leaving the houses and traffic behind to enter the world of fields, horses, geese, chickens, cows and sheep. Beth's long hair danced to the tune of the gentle cool wind as she walked into it and she stuck her hands in the pockets of her fleece jacket more for comfort than warmth. She smiled as she found a packet of Polo mints. She remembered her dad calling them Sunday sweets – holey he said they were. She missed him, had missed him a great deal since his death – it had become easier and she could happily think of him without crying, although sometimes her eyes would well up. A little chuckle graced the air as Beth remembered saying to her dad, "Don't you dare die and leave me here alone with mother," with the wonderful gallows humour they could both enjoy. But he did precisely that. Later she found there were times when she could laugh and say, "I know you're looking down at me and saying, don't you dare send her up here too soon! I think you are safe...she doesn't seem to have any intention of dying...I reckon it's her mission to outlive me." More recently she had been able to say, "Having fun up there, you two?" She would remember, with girlish giggles, watching the undertaker trying to gently make the grave look smooth after interring her mother's ashes in her father's grave, and having to resort to whacking the shovel down on the earth to do so. He knew he shouldn't, but he couldn't help but laugh when Beth, thus far unnoticed by him, quietly said, "That's probably dad letting you know he isn't ready yet to have her interrupting his resting place – he's been enjoying himself."

Simon had come to know Beth a little, having conducted the funeral arrangements for her dad and husband previously, and now her mum. He joked back at her, "Ah, Mrs. Channing...one of my favourite customers...I told you last time that I didn't want to see you again, but mum had other ideas eh?"

Beth knew the village roads well and regularly walked them, a pursuit opportune for clear thinking and she really needed that now. What would James make of what she had written? Would he show Hazel?

"Hello Goliath, hello Lottie," Beth called out as she put her elbows over the top bar of the gate, leaned against it and waited for the shire horse and the donkey to come for her to stroke their heads. Both being very sociable creatures they made themselves known to anyone who was passing and they loved to interact with people. Beth had been one of their 'pets' for many years now and she had toyed with the idea of writing stories about the equine pair, although quite how to do it hadn't yet revealed itself. Crime was her style of writing but somehow a murderous donkey or a bank-robbing shire horse, or the obvious drugs mule, even though potential storylines, didn't bring flowing ideas. Goliath seemed to amble across the field, his great strides meaning Lottie had to trot to keep up with him if she was to reach their pet human at the same time as her huge companion. This time Goliath won and he stood across the width of the gate so that when Lottie arrived she couldn't reach Beth. Poor Lottie tried to nuzzle in without success so she delivered an ear-numbing bray of admonition directed at Goliath. He moved.

"Oh, Lottie, you speak out without fear, why can't I do it? I've done something which should have been done long ago but to admit my innermost feelings and thoughts was...is...so hard. Can I tell you what I've done? Of course I can. You aren't going to tell anyone. Well, you know James? And you know how he and I have this...this...this closeness between us, and you know how Hazel is jealous of it and openly tries to turn his head? She's done it again. Do you remember me telling you about all those past life dreams I have had? Yes, I know I'm a bit weird but it wasn't my request for all this stuff to be revealed to me." As she stroked them Goliath and Lottie both moved their heads as if in a nod of agreement. Beth carried on rubbing their heads and continued, "Well, I decided to write it all down and let James know. He is already aware I have had these dreams but I could never tell him the full details. Now he will know everything...that all of them portray the eternal triangle through the centuries and that the three souls have always been him, Hazel and me. Can you help me, guys? Can you tell me if I have done the right thing?"

The two animals, as though they had listened intently and understood every word she had spoken, pushed their heads a little closer as if offering a hug.

"Thanks you two. Thank you for letting me offload. Maybe the answer will come to me before I get home," she said, and in unison Lottie and Goliath took a step back and dipped their heads as if to say, "It was our pleasure to listen. Go and find your answer."

With fond farewells made Beth resumed walking along the lane, past the honking geese and Home Farmhouse, all the while churning over recurrent thoughts. One minute she was glad she had set out everything for James to read and the next it felt as though she had pushed the red button launching a warhead. What was the worst that could happen? He could want her to stop all contact with him...yes, that was the worst thing...but what could be the best thing to happen? He could understand every word of it. What had she actually said? And, maybe more importantly, why had she said it? As she walked the stresses were melting away and she was feeling calm and even considered making plans for the future but just for now, right now, she was going to thoroughly enjoy her walk. Tomorrow was another day for making plans. The rural road wasn't used very much by traffic, except for the mornings and evenings when locals were going to or returning from work but even then it wasn't overly used. Used just enough to make everyone careful and to be aware of what might be coming around the corner or behind them. It was certainly quiet enough to hear anything approaching. She heard a tractor in the distance and as she scanned the landscape she spotted it two fields away, going about its business in an unhurried fashion. Not far away were the trees which sheltered a couple of cottages from view and Beth's spirits did a little dance as she realised what was beyond them...5

minutes and she would be there. She thought of Charlotte and of her friend from pre-school days, George, wondering if they would be able to meet up as planned at the weekend. George was going to drive to Southampton this time as Charlotte had travelled to Nottingham last time. They both seemed to be doing well at their respective universities – it would be interesting to witness their lives unfold before them, just as she was able to see Daniel's and Emily's lives open up and lead them ahead. An image of her dad came to mind and she whispered, "Hello, dad. Nice to have you with me – I do miss you, you know. Perhaps you do know and that's why you are coming to see me so much."

Before she knew it, Beth could see the little bridge and immediately after that would be the place she loved. The road was straight and she could see it, the wide verge where she stood to watch the water tumble over the weir. Sanctuary.

The car quickly gathered speed as it accelerated behind her. "Idiot!" thought Beth. "Just because it is a straight road drivers think they can do whatever speed they want." She stood off the road on to the verge for safety. As she turned she saw, with terror in her eyes, that the car was aiming straight for her, making no attempt to go safely past her. The force of the crash flung Beth into a tree about 15ft away, her back taking the impact. She ricocheted off the trunk and landed in a twisted heap, on the way to unconsciousness and in excruciating pain. She heard the car screech to a halt and was aware of a figure walking back towards her. The person leaned over her and Beth put an arm up for help but, instead of receiving it, hands curled around her throat and squeezed hard. Satisfied at the lifeless form at their feet, the silent person walked back to the car and drove away.

It was not the right time of day for much traffic but Lady Luck was shining one small ray of light on Beth's still form. It might have been a small ray but it had the biggest impact ever in the shape of a cyclist in the full battle gear of Lycra and helmet who hurriedly backtracked when he realised that what he had just passed was a body. Full of dread, he knelt beside her and, remembering basic first aid, put his ear by her nose and mouth...and felt the gentlest of breaths. She was alive but cold. He dialled 999, then set about making the barely conscious woman as comfortable as he dared, talking to her all the while, knowing that hearing was the last sense to leave the body. He was rewarded by a soft guttural moan and continued to reassure her that she was not going to be left alone and an ambulance was on its way, all the while praying with every passing second that she would not die. Not expecting answers he introduced himself as Peter and continued to chat about anything and everything, looking all the time for changes in Beth's state and looking for clues as to who she was. He picked up the phone which he could see just underneath her arm. Peter found one single message which said, 'Please call if you need anything – ever.' He saw it had been received long ago, yet had been kept; this person must be important to the badly injured woman now in his care.

The voice at the end answered, "Hello, Beth. I'm so pleased to hear from you – I was afraid I might not..." and Peter cut in to explain all that he could and before the conversation ended he knew that someone called James was already in his car and on his way to the weir.

The policeman was talking to Peter when James appeared and the very welcome sound of the ambulance's siren announced its arrival a few minutes later. It was whilst the medics were working hard on Beth and making her stable for conveyance to hospital that one of them called for attention from the policeman. Alerted by the tone of the voice, James and Peter watched and listened as bags were secured around her hands. The two men felt equally helpless as they watched injections given, intravenous lines set up and a mask put over Beth's white face. Her legs, so badly twisted, had to be straightened and splinted. Her spine, clearly compromised, required delicate and specialist handling. It seemed to take forever before the crew were ready to put Beth in the ambulance but neither man wanted to leave until they saw her on her way to hospital. Just before setting off, one of the medics spoke to them both, to thank Peter for his efforts in assisting Beth before they arrived, and to tell them both that there was no doubt Beth would be taken straight to theatre. They had all the information they needed so there was no need for either of them to follow them...tomorrow would be quite soon enough to make telephone enquiries regarding possible visits.

James let out a howl of despair, screaming, "No! No! No! No! I must go with her...don't take her without me...No! No!" he persisted as he watched the ambulance drive away, blue lights flashing and siren signalling the urgency of its journey.

"Sir, calm down! Sir! Sir! Stop!" tried the police officer, all to no avail, as James could not be hushed. No-one knew his past so couldn't have possibly known that he was reliving the moment when he heard of Laura's death. Only when he broke down in tears did he hear the policeman telling him that he would drive him to the hospital – he was in no fit state to drive himself.

Peter went on his way, knowing that in the morning one of the first things he would do was find out how Beth Channing was, and that the last thing he would do that night would be to pray that she survived all that lay ahead of her.

Peter's prayers were answered and Beth survived the lengthy surgery required to her spine, two broken legs and a broken pelvis; he was relieved and decided to visit in a couple of days' time happy now to carry on with his daily life and, of course, he would telephone again in the evenings to follow her progress. James stayed 36 hours at the hospital, waiting for Beth to come out of surgery, hoping then to be told that he could see her. The second part of his hopes was not granted; Beth was taken to the intensive care unit where a policeman sat outside the door. However, she was deemed well enough to be moved on Saturday morning and put in a side ward on her own where she had a constant visitor. James went home on Friday morning to shower, sleep and change his clothes and Hazel stayed the night with him, happy to help him deal with his anxiety. She was really attentive and happy to help.

When James finally surfaced on Saturday Hazel said, "I let you sleep because you looked like you needed it and I've rung the hospital. They are not allowing her to have visitors...not until Monday."

Hazel stayed again on Saturday night, and Sunday night.

So it was Monday when James took the afternoon off work and raced to the hospital, all but fell into Beth's room and found it full of cards, vases of flowers, a balloon, and a woman he didn't know. Beth looked at the woman and said quietly, "Rachael, this is James; James, this is Rachael

McGoldrick."

Before James could say a syllable Rachael jumped in with, "Ah...hello James. Nice to meet you at last...I hear you stayed here until Beth came out of surgery."

"Hello, Dr. McGoldrick...it's good to meet you, too. This looks awful Beth. How long will it take for you to mend? Dr? Can you tell me anything? I've been so worried about you Beth," he replied, adding, "Who sent you the beautiful flowers and balloon?"

When he heard that Alison and Lavinia had brought the carnations in on Saturday and Peter had brought the balloon and the irises on Sunday James felt rather perplexed and it showed. Rachael noted the expression on his face but said nothing.

"Rachael, would it be OK if I could speak with James alone, please?" Beth asked, and Rachael left the room to sit behind the nurses' station where she could still see the side room and monitor the visits of anyone who came to see Beth. Not that she was worried about James – there was something about this man that conveyed genuine care for Beth, but Rachael would still keep her senses alerted to what would pass between them. It would be interesting to see what happened. The only people who knew about the attempted strangulation were the doctors and the police...not even Beth knew. Her memory could only take her up to starting off on her walk; not particularly helpful in catching whoever had done this, thought Rachael, but a blessing for Beth.

"Have you read my letter?"

James heard the question but had no idea what Beth was talking about so could only answer, "Letter? Um...no...I haven't seen..."

Beth continued without hearing the rest of his sentence. "I sent it because it should help you understand more. The last time we met you asked me to forgive you. I don't think it will happen, James. The letter should leave you in no doubt that there is a reason as old as time not to forgive you. Can you find a way around that? Because I don't think it is possible. It is my fault I allowed you to have your fun with me so the blame is not entirely yours, but more than once you decided to tell Hazel what you had done or, more precisely, nearly done; did you never once think how peculiar it was that she always stayed with you? This last time you told her even when you knew that she would blacken my name through the village, and then you cut me completely from your life with not a word or care as to what you had done. Yet you knew what she would do and what the repercussions would be for me. I was stonewalled by you and, true to what you said, my name was, indeed, blackened. You did nothing except hang me out to dry, and now you ask for my forgiveness? I told you once that you had my forgiveness always but what you did was a step too far. In three lifetimes I allowed you to succeed, the pair of you...in this lifetime you are both trying again to crush me completely. I forgive you for the three lives past, but not this time. Not after that."

The damage to Beth's throat had now reduced her voice to little more than a hoarse whisper and the difficulty in speaking was reflected by her face.

Concern now rising sharply in James, his reply came out louder and harsher than intended. "Beth...what are you talking about? I don't follow everything you are saying."

She grimaced, drew in a long slow breath and paced her reply to match her fading energy levels. "You said I'm special to you. I'm not. Only in the sense that I have been a pawn who you got to play into the hands of both of you. And she kept taking you back because she needed me in your life. What happened when I wasn't included in your life? How were things between you? Why did you ask to meet me again after so long?"

His concern was fast crossing the line into fear, regret, and desperate awful realisation as he replied in an equally measured voice, "I missed you, Beth, missed you a lot. I missed your wit, I missed your conversation, I missed your smile, your personality, I missed...uh...I...um...missed you. I realise now that Hazel couldn't give me what you did...when you were around my life seemed perfectly all right." James paused, gathering his thoughts to say something important. "I'm a selfish bastard, aren't I? I'm so very sorry."

Beth dug deep into her reserves of strength – this was important, their futures depended on it. "What you were getting from me, James, is what was feeding her and when I wasn't around her supply had vanished. The two of you were sucking the life out of me, just like you did three times before. No, you aren't sorry yet because you haven't fully realised what is going on, and probably won't until you finish reading my letter. You are going to have to make a decision as to what to do about Hazel. You will have to decide whether to go forward with her soul into future lives, or you are going to have to find a way to cut that link between you. Now, please leave me to rest, I am very tired. Really tired. Tired of everything. Best of luck with your thinking." And Beth closed her eyes to end the communication between them.

James asked with quiet desperation, "What letter? I've not seen a letter from you." At receiving no reply he hung his head low then stood and leaned over to kiss Beth's forehead. Instinct threw her eyes open and she tried to scream, pure terror etched on her face. "Dr!...Rachael!...Rachael...it's Beth...help, please," yelled James, unable to keep the panic from his voice and actions.

She was beside Beth in an instant ready to catch her flailing arms and calm her down. He fired off a load of questions, "What's happening to her? Did I do something? What have I done? Shall I leave? Can I stay?" Rachael called the nurses to attend Beth and she took James to a private room where she placed a pocket dictaphone on the table and sat back.

"What is going on?" James asked. "Why are you recording our conversation?" He was totally bewildered, a reaction not unnoticed by Rachael.

"I am not a doctor," said Rachael. "I am Detective Sergeant McGoldrick, and I have been assigned to protect Mrs. Channing." She spoke into the recorder, "It is 15:05 on Monday, 16 October 2017. Present in the room are James Richardson and Detective Sergeant Rachael McGoldrick."

James could not hold back. "Protect Beth? What do you mean protect her? Why?"

"We protect anyone who we suspect is the victim of attempted murder," Rachael answered. "This is not a formal interview..."

James interrupted, incomprehension obvious in his voice. "Murder? You think someone ran her down on purpose? But why?"

Rachael carried on, not answering him. "This is merely to record what is said between us. You are not under suspicion...we know you were working when Beth was knocked over and left for dead."

"Then what do you want with me Rachael? Uh...am I allowed to call you Rachael? Should I call you something else if this is police business? Why did she react like that when all I wanted to do was kiss her goodbye? I don't understand," ended James, sounding lost and utterly miserable but knowing, at long last, how important having Beth in his life was.

"Rachael is fine, James. I have a photograph to show you...do you recognise this at all?"

"What has this got to do with Beth's accident?"

"It was found in Beth's hand when the ambulance crew were tending to her. We think she grabbed it when whoever ran her down probably also tried to strangle her," said Rachael, letting the impact of her words sink in.

"STRANGLE?" exclaimed James, and then "Strangle?" in a tone of total disbelief. "No! Not Beth! Who would want to kill her? No...no...can't be." But as he said it doubts flooded in as he thought about how Hazel had been since the accident...overly attentive? And the fact that she told him that Beth could have no visitors until today...clearly untrue! And what letter? Where was it? "Rachael, whoever did this, you find them and you throw the key away. Do you hear me? Throw the key away!"

He knew. James at last knew. It had taken a long, long time, but now he knew everything. "I see you, Beth, I know who you are. I'm not leaving you again." He didn't realise he had said it out loud.

CHAPTER NINETEEN

With happily given help from friends, some old, some new, Beth made steady progress with her recovery but she needed a focus. Simply wanting to get well again was not enough – there had to be something else too, because concentrating on one thing alone was never a good idea as it led to dissatisfaction, disappointment and lack of progress. That something else, Beth decided, was to start writing again. It was no good, she could just not get her head in the right place for anything much these days but at last she had now made the decision to finally do something positive. Those new anti-depressants must be working really well to have brought her to make that decision and now she wanted to be strong enough to follow it through.

"Don't lose the faith now!" Beth thought to herself. "The darkness will take over again if I don't do something. I must make a list of what I want to say to my doctor and include the need to get back into writing."

So, with pen, paper and a hopeful mind she made her list of questions and 'matters arising' for her very understanding doctor to digest the next day.

Much to her surprise she was still upbeat about her idea as she discussed her plans with Dr. Jacobson and he listened intently, very aware that with everything that had happened to his patient in recent weeks she would need a little more help than he, or any anti-depressants, could give her. The road ahead was almost vertical. The courage of this woman had hit a chord with the doctor and they had forged a good, strong, patient/doctor relationship. Yes, he would find it easy to suggest a next step for her to consider.

"Beth, please don't disregard this out of hand, but have you thought of talking to, say, a psychotherapist to help you? There is a doctor who would be very good for you if you would like to take that route; he works at the other practice in town and I know him quite well. He has specialised in the field of the mind and all appointments are conducted on a private basis in his own home. He runs it in tandem with his GP job." Dr. Jacobson ventured and then fell silent as he waited for Beth to answer.

"A psychoperson? Oh, I don't know," she began, defensively.

"I understand your fears, but I will tell you that Dr. Hunter is a very nice man, a little older than me, and he has a great success rate to his credit. A family man, he has three grown-up children which, no doubt, would give you some common ground. The prefix 'psycho' is still terrifying, even in this day and age but, you know, it really is just another word. Look, here are his details. Give it some thought and then, when you are ready, give him a ring. If anyone can sort you out, he will," finished Dr. Jacobson with a look of gentle persuasion.

Beth slowly took the information, thanked him for his suggestion and promised she would think about it seriously.

Her friend, Anne, listened to the account of her appointment with the GP as they sat in Beth's kitchen with a cup of tea, and watched her play with the card she held in her hands, twisting it this way and that, tracing it through her fingers until at last she stopped and stared at it.

"Oh, Anne, I don't know what to think," she puffed out, sounding at her wit's end. "I know it doesn't mean I'm a nutcase but, I don't know, do you think this stuff works or is it more like a load of mumbo jumbo designed to fleece you of your money?"

Anne sat forward in her chair, straightened her back and placed clasped hands on the table. She let out a breath then lifted her eyes to meet Beth's and said, "Well, dear, I think you have a valid point there but this man is a GP and has been recommended by a GP who you've known for a long time. It strikes me that this recommendation is more than likely sound. Why don't you ring Dr. Hunter and have a chat with him, put forward your fears and concerns, and see where it goes from there? You have nothing to lose and, perhaps, everything to gain."

"You are right Anne, I know you are. I've been holding on to this card for days now. Would you be OK to drive me to an appointment if I make one, please?"

Beth regarded her friend as not just older but a lot wiser than herself and felt safe as Anne readily and happily assented to taking her to as many appointments as she wanted her to, at the same time passing the telephone to Beth. She knew that look on her friend's face and it said, 'action.'

"Please stay, Anne, and help me out here if I need it," Beth asked quietly as she began to punch out the number, half hoping that no-one was at the other end to answer her call. A male voice, however, answered "Good morning. Paul Hunter speaking," which for a couple of very long seconds threw Beth off balance. Stuttering that she would like to speak to Dr. Hunter brought the reply she dreaded, "Speaking...how may I help?" After a shaky start she got across all she wanted to say without any interruption from him and she received a reply she really was not expecting. And so it was arranged that, as he was to be passing her door that afternoon and if it was agreeable to her, he would call in at 2:30pm and they could go through her queries in more detail. Anne said she would stay if Beth felt awkward about it and that was more than acceptable to all three of them.

Sure enough, at the appointed time the doorbell rang. Beth heard Anne's voice. "Hello, you must be Dr. Hunter. Please come in."

And then a man's voice saying, "And you must be Anne...thank you. Mrs. Channing said she had mobility difficulties so I have presumed you are Anne. Please excuse me if I am speaking out of turn."

Anne smiled broadly, quite taken with the man now making his way through to the lounge to see Beth. He noticed the wheelchair folded neatly away but said nothing. If this lady wanted to tell him, she would. She didn't. Happy with what she heard from Dr. Hunter she agreed to try his psychowhatever and an appointment was made. Next Wednesday she hoped to be on the first step to a focused recovery and then she could set about feeling better about herself because she would be getting somewhere. It was going to be a long week and she hoped she would not change her mind.

There is always the proverbial fly in the ointment and one had decided to make its way into Beth's plans. Whereas she had been feeling quite positive about looking at the causes of her lack of writing abilities, today was a different matter entirely. The high had turned into a low and that affected everything including the desire to get out of bed. The downward spiral was about to consume her; she had long since given up trying to stop it. When this happened she just gave in and let it take its course – it would be over later, or tomorrow, or maybe not for several days. If only her legs would work! The pain wasn't quite so bad now in that it wasn't every hour of every day any more, but that failed to register in the positive side of Beth's brain on days like today. She sighed in emotional defeat and drifted back into sleep only to be woken by a telephone call from Frankie. If only Frances knew how well timed that call had been.

"Hi, Beth. I'm at Waitrose picking up some lovely ham, cheese, salad stuff, and freshly baked bread to bring over to you for lunch – I'm inviting myself to your house. What would you like for dessert?" asked her ever-energetic friend.

A very flat sounding Beth replied, "Thank you, it will be nice to see you. I don't mind what dessert is...you choose. You'll have to take me as you find me today – sorry."

Perceptive as ever, Frankie recognised the signs but remained her cheerful self and chose two desserts; she knew that Beth's choice could go one of two ways, depending on how far down the scale she had fallen so far. Strawberries and clotted cream would be perfect for one end and a heavily iced chocolate cupcake with double cream would suit the other. "Please let it be a strawberry day," muttered Frankie as she stopped her car outside Beth's house, but her heart sank on seeing the curtains were only opened a little way. "Oh, no!" she softly groaned, lifting the shopping out of the car as she did so. "She was doing so well. Cupcakes and double cream here we come."

Cupcakes and double cream worked their magic.

CHAPTER TWENTY

Reading finished, Megan turned to a drawer and pulled out a bundle of papers and Mayrie could not disguise the gasp of total disbelief at what she saw. The front page read "Consider This." Gran didn't seem that surprised but there was something she needed from all this, something Mayrie didn't yet comprehend.

Megan was first to speak. "We thought this was what you were talking about, Amber. Dad had a copy. Because we were too young at the time he gave it to his mum and dad with instructions for it to be kept but, of course, over the years it was packed up and put away – firstly in gran and granfer's belongings and then in mine. It was only last year when James came to live with me and we had a jolly good clear-out to make room for his things that it came to light. It has bothered us lately and we wondered if we should come to you with it; perhaps we were picking up on what was going on with you. We have always loved you, Amber, and we are not going to say or do anything to hurt you, which is why we need to be really sure you want to look at this."

Gran reached out and held their hands and simply said, "Mayrie doesn't know what it really is and yes, please, I am ready to face it again. There is much I have to lay to rest. But there is something I need you to listen to also," and she played the recording of the conversation between their dad and Rachael.

It took a while, but Amber, James and Megan gently explained to Mayrie how it was all true...that it was a factual account of their father's and Amber's mother's life. Beth was Amber's mum, Debbie; James was their dad, Andrew Lindley; Holly was the cover for the both of them; Daniel and Charlotte were, in fact, Jack and Amber. Hazel was someone called Bridget. And, yes, the shorter story was completely true in every way. Peter and Max were real, Rachael McGoldrick was real, and the details of the hit and run and attempted murder were real.

"The videos, gran...that was...?" Mayrie's voice trailed off, "and ...Oh, gran! All that stuff that Roshan is working on...this is AWESOME."

James then laughed and, with the look of a naughty schoolboy, fetched an old photograph album and said, "Mayrie, be prepared to meet your great-grandmother as you may not have seen her before. Dad took these pictures so I don't think anyone else has these."

As the first page was turned Mayrie and Amber saw two lovely pictures, one of a woman and one of a man, and

Mayrie realised what the familiar feeling was that she had experienced on arrival at James and Megan's house. Megan bore a striking resemblance to her father. The two photographed characters were Andrew and Debbie and they looked so right there together on the page. Over the pages images of James and Megan as children appeared, there were even a few of Amber looking about 20 years old, but then came something that stunned her. A photograph with the caption 'My Biker Girl' almost leapt out of 2D to become 3D. It was Debbie, long hair flowing in the breeze, wearing skinny black jeans and a black leather jacket which stopped at the waist.

"I remember telling her to stop looking like that," said Amber. "But she looked absolutely stunning, didn't she? She wasn't young, you know, when that was taken." The day was full of memories, chatter, and confessions. Amber, through many tears of relief, sadness and joy, told of how she and Jack didn't like Andrew very much because they saw how he upset their mum. It later became clear how and why, and its name was Bridget...but she felt it was because of their dislike of him that she and Andrew never married. They didn't accept him for a long time. The bigger confession though came from Andrew through James and Megan.

"Amber, there is something else you should see. I have no doubt now; do you James? There can be a no more right time than now. This, Amber, is for you, written by dad shortly before he died."

Megan handed her an envelope. After staring at it for a moment or two Amber opened it and read:

"Dear Amber and Jack, There is so much I should have liked to say to you, to explain to you, but I acknowledge, accept and understand all that went between us over the years. Thank you for eventually accepting me in your mum's life. I love her, you know...always did and always will...I was just too much of an idiot to see it...and I was scared. I was scared of getting in the way of the memories of James and Megan's mum and your dad, and I didn't want your relationship with your mum to suffer because of me. I have left the draft of a book written by your mum with James and Megan and our stories are in there. You, Jack, were the boy sent to the gladiatorial arena and you, Amber, were the boy on the ship. In both cases my soul was too weak to stand against the circumstances of the time and I let both of you and your mother down in the worst possible way. She was mother to each of you at those respective times. The soul of the queen and that of the person who steered me away from the tavern girl was the same and that soul also cropped up in this life. You will remember Bridget? It was her. We were all brought together in this lifetime for a purpose. Each lifetime gives us the opportunity to redress any wrongs done before and this was my time to make it right with your mum but, much to my enduring shame, I missed the chance. What my soul had done previously was dreadful to say the very least and it took a very long time for me to accept the past. It is hard to know how bad one has been. I prayed that one day you would see beyond the past and allow me to create a future, and you did. Thank you so very much, from the bottom of my heart.In this envelope you will find a few photos. These are of Debbie and me, Peter and Max, Rachael and Frances at the weir, which held a particular significance to us all. They were taken on the day of the summer solstice 2019...the day I made a vow to your mum...also the day I knew I had lost her love. It never stopped me loving her, nevertheless. My behaviour to Debbie was nothing short of appalling, blinded as I allowed myself to be by another and by the time I did what I should have done it was too late and I had irreversibly hurt your mum's heart – again. My arrogance and, as she so correctly said, my desire for self-punishment, prevented me from recognising her and all that had gone before. My acknowledgement was too late, far too late. We made a peace between us and our life is now full of affection. It has been an absolute honour to be given the chance to continue caring for her through our remaining years. My heart aches for each one, with only myself to blame. I would like to think there will be future lifetimes when I can redress what I so cruelly got wrong this time and in previous times, and for my part in the histories which affected the souls of you, Amber and Jack, and your mum, I am sorry to the core. One day I hope to earn forgiveness for all of that. Thank you for what we have already achieved in that direction.You two and my two are the best children anyone could wish to have hoped for, each of you a perfect testament to your respective mother's love, devotion and characters. I love you all, always did, and hope beyond hope, that you get everything you want out of life. Don't ever give up. Take it. Live it. Regret nothing. Fondest love, Andrew

Amber looked at the second page, cleared her throat and asked Mayrie to read for them all to hear:

Love of my soul, you stood by me all these centuries past. I cannot describe how it feels to stand here with you to declare my eternal devotion, gratitude, love and so much more. My feelings for you are deeper than the deepest ocean and as true as our need to breathe. Without you at my side I am nothing. Sri Yogananda wrote, "Only that which is the other gives us fully unto ourselves." You complete me – you are my "other."I ask the sun to shine on my words, the water and the breeze to carry them for the world to hear, and for the trees to dance to the song in my heart as I say to you, Debbie, my soul's one true love, my love for you will never fade and it is with joy and, at last, peace that I pledge my eternal devotion to you. I promise to love, be true and protect you until the end of time. I know what love is now; it is you.

The silence was a complete stillness as Mayrie finished reading until she whispered "Powerful." She'd just experienced a compassion she had never felt before and, looking rapidly from one to the other, she saw that gran, James and Megan all had tears in their eyes. "We didn't know that part," Megan stated simply.

"I don't know what to say," said James.

Amber's wavering voice added, "They were meant to be together – I wish I had seen it from the start."

"Maybe you did," suggested Megan. "Don't forget your dad was terminally ill when our dad was on the scene; it could have seemed like he was going to be a replacement. And then you left home for university so, again, it probably looked like he was poised to take over your place too. Also, that woman, Bridget, had a lot to answer for...she manipulated him and he hurt your mum several times – emotionally, I mean. Oh, goodness me! He could not have swatted a fly – in fact, he never did...he was so kind and gentle."

"He was," interjected James.

Mayrie's next words were more like a question than a statement. "Andrew's words – they sounded as if he knew he was going to die." If anyone knew the answer to that, it wasn't forthcoming. Amber managed a watery smile and told them that remembering what she felt towards Andrew at the beginning was making her very sad and wished she could go back and change things, be nicer to him. She had subsequently come to adore him but that is what made her so sad – the time wasted and the misdirected negativity she had hurled at him. It was Mayrie who surprised them all, including herself, by explaining that as one of the children who had died in a previous lifetime she was obviously tuning into what had happened but wasn't aware of it, and that is why she disliked him. She was afraid he was going to repeat history and hurt her mum so heinously all over again, and the same must have been true from Jack's perspective. Mayrie excitedly left the room, returning a few moments later with some of Debbie's journals she had brought with her, having chosen them purely on the prettiness of their covers, of all reasons. That had turned out to be a wise decision because amongst them was one for the summer of 2019. The four of them were delighted, but also sad, to find Debbie's vow to Andrew. It read:

Andrew, the affection I have for you is true, as I believe your declaration of love for me to be. Thank you for being here for me and for stepping into the future at my side, whatever it may bring. If the wind and water that carry your words and the sun that shines on them have room for my words too, I ask them to also take my heart's hopes and intentions to be kind, understanding and, although I cannot promise to love you again the way I once did, to make our years together joyful for us both.

The rest of the visit with James and Megan was spent reminiscing and catching up and Mayrie was fascinated by all the tales they told from years gone by. But when she and Amber told them about all the things they had found and given to Roshan to bring back to life, James and Megan could barely contain themselves. They had a few things packed away, mainly CDs of their father's music, and so it was arranged for them to go and stay with Amber where all these wonderful things could once more be seen and heard. They all agreed that if only history could have been taught at school like that there would have been many more interested pupils. The stay with James and Megan had only been short but, by the time they left, Mayrie felt she had known them for years and it was an emotional time for each of them as they parted. No matter, they would soon be visiting each other again.Roshan would take a few weeks to complete the task of re-enabling the equipment Amber had found and when one waits for something the time drags interminably. 'Like watching paint dry,' Mayrie had heard her parents say as they waited for either her or her brother to complete something complicated like tidying their bedrooms. Well, Mayrie wasn't prepared to watch paint dry and rather suspected gran wasn't either. This had been an incredible time of discovery for them all and when they returned from Oxford she gave her gran the surprise of her life...if there could be anything greater than the surprises uncovered recently. She ensured gran was happy, unruffled and had a cup of tea and a piece of cake because she was sure that what she had to say would probably be a shock. As gently as she could Mayrie told of how she had been granted extra holiday time – her employers had been very understanding about it all – and of how she had been making arrangements so, if it was all right with her, she was all set up to take her to see Jack and Emily in Canada. All gran had to do was say, "Yes, please," and get ready to go. The display of emotion was of no surprise to either of them – disbelief, excitement, happiness and so many tears of joy. They would wait until Roshan had worked his wizardry on the iPad so they could take it with them for Jack and Emily to share the wonderful memories. If Jack could just see the videos of his mum. Of course, they would take copies of the stories and photographs...so much to do before leaving for Canada.

"I'm on it, gran," called Mayrie as she left for her own home.

Amber took a moment to light a few candles and placed them beside a photograph of her mum with Andrew and felt warm delight and comfort from watching the flames. Like their love, she thought; a flame which burned bright, faltered, burned bright again and carried on until the wick of life ran out. For both of them it had been a short wick and Amber hoped – no! – believed – they would meet again another time, another place, when the life they should have had long ago would at last materialise sometime in the future. She silently pleaded with Spirit that the soul of Bridget would never again, through all eternity, meet theirs. She had created millennia of pain and misery for all of them because of that one deadly sin, envy. Amber thought of her own grandmother and sent another prayer that her soul should not have to bear jealousy again. As Amber gazed at the flames' hypnotic dance memories bubbled to the surface of a time she had almost successfully lost. She was about to revisit one of the most painful periods of her life. It was so, so painful but the memories demanded to be heeded and she allowed herself to be taken on the journey of deep hurt and anguish.Andrew's death was the gateway to so many things including Amber's mother's death a few months later. He had been mortally wounded by an intruder at his home. Although he had moved in with Debbie he had kept his house so that Ray, June, James and Megan would have somewhere to stay during school holidays and weekends for years to come. Fairly soon after he died Debbie had fallen almost the whole way down an escalator with devastating results as previous surgery had been affected and both hips were broken. She had complained of chest pains a day or two earlier but the battery of tests given at the hospital showed her heart to be sound and strong; not finding any reason for the fall, it was deemed to be a case of over-balancing or possibly grief. She had become wheelchair-bound again and did not recover well either physically or mentally, so Amber had returned to England with her husband's blessing to care for Debbie and bring her back to health. It didn't work out that way in the end. Amber sank deeper and deeper into complete relaxation and eventually fell into a dreamlike state.

With their back to Amber, she watched Andrew show something small to the second person in the room. A hand went out to take it but suddenly Andrew's hand closed around it and he turned to put the item in an open drawer. Without warning Andrew was hit hard across his back with something heavy enough to make him buckle, giving the attacker time to swing the object again, this time across his head. He crashed to the floor bleeding and unmoving where another blow was rained down on his head, and a hand quickly found and picked up whatever he had been holding. Amber's dreams relived receiving the news of Andrew's death; he had survived long enough to give hope for some kind of recovery but the day he had said he was not afraid to die was his last day of lucidity. Within hours he had died. With the news of her mother's serious fall there had been no question of what would happen next. Liam's young face was grave and earnest as he told her she was to take the first flight available and go to look after her mother, there was to be no argument and things would work out as they went along, no matter how long it took. She knew without doubt she had married the right man. He sent her off with the promise of following her when he could secure holiday leave...they had no children yet so there was nothing apart from Liam and her employers to worry about. Both had given her instructions to stay with her mother for as long as it took. She arrived to find her mum barely able to walk and in need of round the clock care. This was going to be a long recovery and Amber quickly settled back into the house she had grown up in, happy to have co-carers of Frankie, Anne, Alison, Peter and Max. They worked out a timetable of who would do what and when, with Amber, of course, doing all night care. The gratitude Debbie felt was huge and would have been overwhelming were it not for the grief which she tried to hide. Her grief at losing Andrew was indescribably deep and with learning to walk again being such a slow and painful process it was taking a toll on her resolve to get well. Peter and Max were also getting over Andrew's death but that was the difference – they were getting over it, bit by bit. It was a couple of months before Amber went back to Canada for a short break to spend some precious time with Liam, which pleased Debbie because she didn't want her daughter to wreck her own life on account of her yet at the same time she was glad to have her helping so much with her recovery. How blessed she was to have so many loving people around but Andrew wasn't here and that was one massive hole in her life which seemed to get deeper with every passing week. Debbie looked over her shoulder as she thought she'd heard him say something; "It is all written down. Put the books together." Manoeuvrability was good enough for her to do some things and as long as she paced her energies it was generally workable but she wished the pains in her chest would go away. She asked Peter and Max to help with the task of moving all her journals and books to one place rather than having them scattered around. Andrew was right, their life was all written down, waiting for her to read any time she was ready. He had only completed one journal and there it was, on the shelf with hers where he had put it. She listened to a CD of some music he had composed and then consigned the player to a box for storing because it had upset her. If she wanted to hear any other music she would buy another CD player, one which had not played Andrew's music to her. The candles burned with a flickering light as Amber's stream of new knowledge changed into memories coming through her state of relaxation. Although it was like a hypnotic trance she knew where she was and that it was safe to allow these memories to come back. In fact, it was necessary – the silence told her so. Whatever came forward, even if she wasn't particularly ready for it, she acknowledged she was prepared to take it. And so the memories began.

CHAPTER TWENTY-ONE

The first rays of light seeped through the curtains of Amber's untidy bedroom, bringing the welcome permission to get up and try to shake off the shadows of the night. She made her way to the equally untidy bathroom to splash water over her face before shuffling to the kitchen for a redeeming cup of tea. Surely that would bring her into a world giving some form of normality today. She was tired. The dream that night had been of someone in a lead coffin with the lid replaced by a veil thick enough to prevent her from seeing who it was although it was obviously male. The silence accompanying the image said so. Her mum had often talked about 'unspoken knowledge' and Amber now understood completely, without reservation, what she had meant. The only way she could describe it to anyone else was to call it truth, or Spirit, leaving a business card with no return address. When these things happened it meant verifying or unscrambling the message was going to be difficult. It was never simple but to have a mind adept at the cryptic made it slightly easier. Bleary eyed and with the sanity-giving mug of tea in hand, Amber stepped over the book that had fallen from the bookshelf, switched on her iPad, called up her photographs and chose her favourite one of her mother. Debbie smiled back from the screen, that wide and almost mischievous smile that made everyone feel relaxed in her company, her hair blowing gently across her face. That hair. Whatever colour was it? Not one colour, that was sure. Some would pay a lot of money to have hair like that. There were colours ranging from burnt copper to blonde mingling, merging, with none looking out of place because together they made a whole colour.

"Mum, help," were the only two words Amber spoke as she stared at the picture for longer than it took to drink her tea. She was numb and the previous day had been hard, with the night even harder. A little over 24 hours ago Amber had found her mother dead in bed – and it felt like a week ago. Her brother would be home from Canada soon...maybe she would feel better then. There were three weeks left of his contract and, at Amber's insistence, he was staying to finish it before coming home. There was nothing to do that she couldn't manage and Frankie's help was invaluable. She headed for the bathroom, tripping over a book on the way, stepped into the shower and let her tears be disguised by the water washing away the night. Quite how long she stayed in the shower was not really important but she knew it had been a long time and the realisation that she was sitting with her head resting on folded arms across her knees, the hot waterfall beating over her, brought with it the memory of howling, "Why, mum? Why did you die?" All else thereafter remained a mystery. Like a robot, Amber dressed, picked at a breakfast of toast and Marmite, and set off for Frankie's house. With heavy legs Amber willed herself to Frankie's door and waited for it to open; it had not occurred to her that her mum's friend might not be there. She heard the bolt go back, the handle turn and Frankie was there, kind, warm, gentle and soft, and immediately Amber broke down, crying.

"Auntie Frances, I am so unhappy."

Taking Amber's hand and placing an arm around her shoulder, Frankie silently guided her indoors, sat beside her on the sofa and hugged her tightly. "Oh, my dear! You have not called me Auntie Frances for a long time. Take your time and cry as much as you like," she cooed, her eyes full of concern gazing into the room as she waited for as long as it would take, very gently rocking this precious young woman who had turned to her for help. The wracking sobs eased and Amber leaned against her mother's friend until she felt ready to speak. In a voice laden with grief and disbelief she asked, "What's happening, Frankie? Why did she die?"

"I don't know, my love...I don't know anything at the moment. I feel as bewildered as you do," answered Frankie as she mentally finished off the sentence with and you didn't call me Auntie Frances again which means you have regained some strength. "All I know is the same as you, that your mum has gone, leaving a huge space in our lives and there is nothing we can do except wait until the post mortem is completed. You are so young to have to face this – thank you for asking me to help – your trust in me means so much, and always has. Do you know how much it meant to me that when I first became friends with your mum both you and Jack treated me like another mum?" Amber blew her nose again, sat up straight and looked Frankie straight in the eye to say, "We have always loved you, Frankie, simple as that. How long did they say the post mortem would take? Can you remember? Everything is so fuzzy today that I can't remember anything I have been told. Perhaps I just don't want to remember. I can't believe she's gone." They chatted for a long time covering just about everything under the sun, and Frankie explained as gently as she could that the coroner would release his findings as soon as possible as unexplained deaths were always investigated quickly to rule out, or confirm, foul play. She carefully wrapped up that statement in the chit chat so that Amber was not put under more strain than necessary but at the same time making sure that she understood. Amber stayed with Frankie for lunch and returned home, such as it felt at the moment, to occupy herself with some sort of tidy up. Lord knows, she needed to do something and she really needed to stop tripping over books! She wasn't doing particularly well in her endeavours when the doorbell rang so she was not upset to have to leave what she was doing or, more precisely, trying to do.

It was a familiar voice, which said, "Hello, Amber. I am Rachael McGoldrick, I think you will remember me...I am the police officer who was involved in the case of your mother's accident...we met a couple of times."

"Yes," Amber replied. "I remember. I thought you had given up on that."

The policewoman's tone was pleasant but very businesslike as she said, "I wonder if PC Lucas and I might come in – I need to ask you some questions?"

"Yes, of course," answered Amber quietly as she invited them into the kitchen where she offered them a cup of tea, which was accepted gratefully. "What did you want to ask? I thought I'd told the other policemen everything they wanted to know."

PC Lucas took out his notepad as his superior officer began talking. "I would like to talk about your mother, Amber. Firstly, I have to ask if you have found any notes left by her?"

Amber confirmed that no notes had been found, not yet anyway.

Rachael continued, "How had your mum been feeling recently? Had her health deteriorated? Had she been taking any new medications?"

There were so many questions but all Amber could say was that as far as she had seen her mum had been fairly well, the pain was still bad sometimes but, no, she wasn't aware of any new medications, not even herbal remedies. She had heard her mum complain of chest pains and shallow breathing again but she had mentioned a nasty headache which was unusual. She was getting on well with walking again and she had even spoken of writing another story since having therapy with Dr. Hunter, although she knew it would be a challenge. As far as Amber knew everything was reasonably all right. She had fairly recently lost Andrew, of course, which was a major upset for all of them and especially for Debbie but she gave no reason for anyone to think she was suicidal.

Then Rachael asked how Amber had been feeling about her mum's disability. Had it been a strain for her? Had she found looking after her and living away from her own home stressful? Had it made her feel a little resentful? After all, she was young and was thousands of miles away from her husband? It all fell heavily on her shoulders, didn't it? Amber answered as truthfully as she could. She didn't like seeing her mum in pain and disabled, she was angry for a time that the police had not discovered who had been driving the car that ploughed into Debbie and caused the original problems. Occasionally she had felt a little sad at being away from Liam but they were in contact most days. There was nothing preventing her from returning to Canada for a break whenever she needed or wanted to because she had so much help from Frankie and some of her mum's other friends – Anne, Lavinia, Alison, Peter and Max. Liam had recently been over to England on annual leave and she was due to visit him in a few weeks' time. No, she didn't know of anything that was troubling her mother to any great extent apart from the pain and progress with reablement which, at times, seemed to have reached a halt. Very occasionally she cried when she felt she would never get back to walking unaided but then mum's positive attitude surfaced and she seemed to make a step forward. It was all encouraging really. Rachael then asked, "Is it correct that you were your mum's main carer, Amber? You are the one who lived with her, and the others who helped came in and out? Who was with your mother the evening before her death? You had been out, I believe, so was anyone here with her until you came home?" She became acutely aware that Amber had stiffened before she answered and heard a change in her voice. She hoped with all her heart that it was what she thought and not what she was here to find out.

Amber answered with a slightly pinched tone that Rachael was, indeed, correct in her understanding and that

Frankie had kept her mum company on that evening, helping her to bed and leaving before Amber returned at 10:30pm. That was how it worked, Frankie would make sure Debbie was comfortable in bed with everything she needed around her and then they would chat for a while. Sometimes Debbie would still be using her iPad when Amber returned, sometimes she would be asleep or almost asleep. Amber always checked on her mum before going to bed herself and that night she arrived home to find a note on the table from Frankie saying that Debbie was comfortable and using her iPad, and that Frankie had gone home at 10pm as usual. She had asked her mum if she needed anything and had taken her some water and two co-codamol as she thought her headache was getting worse again.

"I then went to bed and called out 'night mum', to which she answered, 'goodnight darling, may your dreams come true.'" Amber slumped in to tears again, just managing to get out, "That was the last thing she ever said to me." And there it was, the telltale reaction that she had been looking for. Rachael had come to know Debbie and her family quite well through the investigations into the accident, but was far enough away to be objective in this line of questioning.

"I am so sorry to have to question you like this, Amber, but I do have to tell you that we cannot rule out foul play having a hand in your mum's death."

Amber's red eyes met Rachael's with deep realisation as she said, "And that includes me, Frankie and anyone else involved with her care...well, I can tell you that not one of those guys would do anything to hurt mum!" This last statement punched the air with clear conviction.

"We have to follow this course, Amber, and I am afraid I am going to have to ask you to let me have your mother's iPad so that we can check it for any clues or suicide notes..."

Rachael was explaining when she stopped to hear Amber very quietly say, as if to herself, "The iPad...I didn't think to look on the iPad for any letters...how stupid of me..."

"It is difficult for us as well as the families of those who have died in unexpected circumstances, and I am truly sorry for having to do this right now...we may have to do it again at a later date, too. It is horrible, but that is the way it is."

Amber's eyes lifted to meet Rachael's and whispered, "Mum's diary...mum's journal...I'll get it for you – it could be useful to you?"

Rachael asked if there were any more journals covering the time from her first accident as it might give her a good insight as to Debbie's outlook on life – she didn't want to say, mental health.

Standing at the door as the officers left with the selected journals Amber began softly crying again. "I didn't have time to tell her. Liam phoned me in the early hours to say that he had set things in motion for our permanent move back to England. I was going to tell her in the morning. She never knew."

Rachael's reply was that knowing, as they did, Debbie's tenet of spiritual matters it was, perhaps, comforting to think she would now see everything and be helping and guiding from the other side.

Walking back through the room, Amber bent to pick up the journal that had obviously fallen after Rachael had removed the ones she needed and quickly glanced through it. It was not her mother's handwriting and it seemed to be short sentences of unimportant observations, but taped to the inside of the back cover was an earring. She delivered it to Rachael later that afternoon. Amber's meditative vision changed at that disclosure and once again she saw Andrew being struck from behind. If, from the spirit world, her mum could see everything, and knew everything, was she able to get the knowledge of who the attacker was through to one of them so that Andrew's murder could at last be solved and dealt with? Suddenly, yet seamlessly, she was looking once more at the man – yes, definitely a man – in the coffin and this time he was holding an open book. Life can take all kinds of twists and it turned out that both Debbie and Andrew did have a hand in the attacker being brought to justice thanks to the journals they had kept. The police psychologist and profiler had found enough evidence in them to warrant questioning Bridget Williams who, eventually, showed the true nature of her personality. During her interview she had alternated from calm and pleasant into a spitting, snarling demon and back again claiming that, the Police report stated, "Andrew would have been mine if she'd done the decent thing and died – not her! She wouldn't die...she should have died...I tried hard enough! But you see, dear, my hands just weren't strong enough. He was a lovely man...we were meant to be together, I know we were, he knew we were...yes, he definitely loved me more than her. He found my earring at the weir, you know, and he was going to give it back to me; then he said he would tell the police that I had tried to kill that bitch...so he had to go. I couldn't let him do that...no, no, no, no. He had to be stopped...so I caved his head in. That stopped the bastard."

Rachael took a quiet delight in being able to tell Bridget that actually Andrew HAD managed to tell them that after he had gathered enough observations he bought a pair of earrings identical to the one found at the accident, taped one to the journal and then confronted her with the other – it was all documented in his journal as confirmation. Bridget Williams was very soon found guilty of Debbie's hit and run accident and the subsequent murder of Andrew and held indefinitely at a secure prison psychiatric hospital. The ensuing years brought no relief to, or from, Bridget's twisted mind and she remained there for the rest of her life. The painful journey to the very inner depths of Amber's memory was almost over. The last memory to come back was the coroner's ruling on Debbie's death. It had been a truly awful time for everyone and the grief intense. The stages of grief eventually passed...the denial, the anger, the blame and lastly the acceptance. The cause of death was established as takotsubo cardiomyopathy or, more plainly put, a broken heart. Debbie had died of a broken heart following Andrew's death, and it was Bridget's fault. Bridget had finally managed to kill Debbie. She had managed to kill them both. Once more, she had managed to take Andrew away from her. The whole thing had played out yet again...this was the fifth lifetime of Debbie being dealt the ultimate grief. No wonder she had died of a broken heart. Amber gradually came out of her reverie with a multitude of feelings and it took a while for her to realise that the winner was one of deep and true acceptance of those two deaths. The almost pleasant addition was something she had not realised was still needed – she could now fully accept the deaths of her daughter, son-in-law, grandson and husband. Her soul, at last, was peaceful.

CHAPTER TWENTY-TWO

"Hello, gran," called Mayrie as she bounced through Amber's door a couple of days later. "Have you recovered enough from visiting James and Megan to start packing for our visit to Jack and Emily? I've brought some lightweight cases so I can help you start, if you would like me to." She paused, looked at her gran and smiled with a quizzical look in her eyes. "You look different somehow gran – there is definitely something different about you – are you excited? Is that it?"

Amber clutched her granddaughter's hands and said, "Yes, I am excited, and I do feel different." She paused. "And I am going to tell you all about it, but first we need to surround ourselves with all our favourite nibbly bits of food and drinks. It will probably take you up, down, throw you sideways but know this – the things I am about to tell you have freed me from the burden of hiding them deep in my subconscious mind. It is good to feel this free and this is what you are seeing in me."

They sat for hours mulling over all that had been revealed in her candlelight meditation and all the questions it raised for Mayrie. The one thing neither of them could know for sure was if Bridget's soul would be subjected to a spiritual judicial cleanse or whether it would be condemned for eternity. She had not just hurt, she had harmed, even killed, so many incarnations of Debbie, Andrew, Jack, Amber, James and Megan and that must have taken envy out of the realms of hardened jealousy and thrown it squarely into the damnable pit of evil. It was a point they could debate but gran and Mayrie both agreed that the most acceptable outcome would be that Bridget's soul would never cross any of them again. Packing could wait until tomorrow, it was decided, and they chose to spend a little time at a very special place instead. It was a clear day and the sun was still shining through the trees at the weir. As they stood, quietly reflecting on everything, a smile crept across Mayrie's face as she recognised someone there.

"Hello, great grandma; hello, Andrew," she said. "I see you."

"Hear that, Mayrie? Listen," said gran.

Mayrie closed her eyes to hear the tumbling water saying: "It's over, it's over, it's over, it's over..."